THE GOLDEN MAGNET

THE GOLDEN MAGNET

Lewis B. Patten

GUNSMOKE

This hardback edition 2010
by BBC Audiobooks Ltd
by arrangement with
Golden West Literary Agency

Copyright © 1997 by Frances A. Henry.
First appeared under the title "The Man on the Stage"
in *Best Western* (01/53)
All rights reserved.

ISBN 978 1 408 46283 6

British Library Cataloguing in Publication Data available.

Printed and bound in Great Britain by
CPI Antony Rowe, Chippenham and Eastbourne

Lewis B. Patten wrote more than ninety Western novels in thirty years and three of them won Spur Awards from the Western Writers of America and the author himself the Golden Saddleman Award. Indeed, this highlights the most remarkable aspect of his work: not that there is so much of it, but that so much of it is so fine. Patten was born in Denver, Colorado, and served in the U.S. Navy 1933–1937. He was educated at the University of Denver during the war years and became an auditor for the Colorado Department of Revenue during the 1940s. It was in this period that he began contributing significantly to Western pulp magazines, fiction that was from the beginning fresh and unique and revealed Patten's lifelong concern with the sociological and psychological effects of group psychology on the frontier. He became a professional writer at the time of his first novel, *Massacre at White River* (1952). The dominant theme in much of his fiction is the notion of justice, and its opposite, injustice. In his first novel it has to do with exploitation of the Ute Indians, but as he matured as a writer he explored this theme with significant and poignant detail in small towns throughout the early West. Crimes, such as rape or lynching, were often at the centre of his stories. When the values embodied in these small towns are examined closely, they are found to be wanting. Conformity is always easier than taking a stand. Yet, in Patten's view of the American West, there is usually a man or a woman who refuses to conform. Among his finest titles, always a difficult choice, surely are *A Killing at Kiowa* (1972), *Ride a Crooked Trail* (1976), and his many fine contributions to Doubleday's Double D series, including *Villa's Rifles* (1977), *The Law at Cottonwood* (1978), and *Death Rides a Black Horse* (1978). His later books include *Tincup in the Storm Country* (1996), *Trail to Vicksburg* (1997), *Death Rides the Denver Stage* (1999), and *The Woman at Ox-Yoke* (2000).

Denver City in the early days of gold discoveries is the setting for *The Golden Magnet*.

Cole Estes is on his way there to work for Mike Forrest, who has the mail and stagecoach franchises for the boomtown. Travelling with him is Mike's daughter, Norah, returning from school in the East.

Then Mike is murdered, and sabotage by ruthless competitors leaves Norah owner of a line without operating capital . . . until Cole comes up with a daring plan.

THE GOLDEN MAGNET

I

THE MAN ON THE STAGE

This land had lain unchanged over a thousand years, marked only by the game trails, by the buffalo wallows, by the fleeting pause of an Indian village upon its vastness. Now a new scar lay upon it, a two-track road, winding ever westward toward the distant elusiveness of snow-clad mountain ranges. The coach that ran down this rutted road, raising a thin plume of dust behind, was no glittering, yellow-wheeled thing of beauty. Its hardwood sides had weathered to a dingy gray, and the grain stood out from the sandblasting of prairie storm, from the pitiless erosion of mud and water.

The painted legend of ownership, defaced by the same forces that had dimmed the glory of the Troy's first beauty, announced that it belonged to the line of **Forest Overland, Denver City, and Auraria**, or abbreviated, the F. O., D. C., & A. Four passengers rattled about inside the shell of the rocking coach, and of these only Cole Estes still held his temper in check, still could contain the irascibility and ill-humor that a week's jolting travel over the world's roughest roads could engender in even the gentlest of humans.

Another of these four was a young woman. She sat directly across from Cole, and she had fallen into a numbed and exhausted stupor. This merciful unconsciousness robbed her of arrogant imperiousness, of consciousness of her own dazzling beauty, things that were so prominent in her when she was awake. Her long lashes lay against smooth cheeks, and her full lips, relaxed this way, were soft and strangely inviting. Beneath the heavy material of her woolen traveling dress, firm and youthful breasts rose and fell evenly with her breathing. Her knee was warm against Cole's own. Sweat put a shine to her nose and cheeks that oddly increased her attraction for Cole.

He caught himself thinking thoughts about her that were not exactly proper. His gray eyes lost their hardness momentarily, but then he thought: *Sleep only shows her for what she might have been, not for the spoiled and willful brat she is.* His steady glance upon her and these thoughts of his must have penetrated her unconsciousness, for she stirred, moaned softly, and opened her eyes. Cole tactfully turned his glance out of the window and stared moodily at the sameness of rolling grassland, of deep arroyo, of treeless infinity.

He was a big man and sat with an easy relaxation that cushioned him against the shock of the coach, slamming interminably down against reach and bolster. His face could have been called handsome or ugly with equal veracity. It bore no single feature that was fine, being too rugged and hard for that. In the aggregate it showed force of will, strength, and stubbornness. The eyes, gray and direct, could be unfeeling and brutal, yet at times during the journey they had rested on the young woman across from him with an almost unwilling gentleness and a lurking humor, as though her arrogance did not displease him nearly as much as it amused him. Except for this slight hint of gentleness, his was the face of an eagle, and wildness was its singular dominating effect.

He wore rumpled woolen trousers and a buckskin shirt, too tight across broad shoulders that revealed the flexing of long, tough muscles whenever he moved. His hair, cropped short, was curly and reminded you in color of a prime beaver pelt. Now he became aware of the low talk between the raw-boned Missouri farmer, Hobart, and Schoonover, the merchant from Boston.

12

"Gold," said Hobart, "is all there is in this stinking country that is worth a man's time."

"Commerce is important," reiterated Schoonover pompously. "There is more profit in that than in grubbing a stream for gold."

It was an argument that had gone on, intermittently but steadily nevertheless, ever since the stage had left Leavenworth. Cole Estes felt a touch of impatience. He said: "Grubbing a stream for gold is productive, and commerce supplies the producers. Both are necessary. Let each man do what he is fitted for, and why argue it out hour after hour?"

The young woman, Norah Forrest, gave this talk her attention, obviously out of sheer boredom, yet she also gave the impression of keeping herself apart, and her air was haughty. She asked, needling Cole: "And what do you think you are fitted for, Mister Estes?"

He put his glance fully upon her, and his thought was plain on his face: *Fitted for taking some of that childish snobbery out of you, perhaps, if I had the time and the opportunity.* But he only said: "Fitted for what I'm doing, which is to ride this rattletrap into Denver and take the job that is waiting for me."

Already he found himself regretting the obligation he had taken on. He thought: *If this coach is a fair sample of Mike Forrest's stageline, then he did some tall lying in his letter. If his daughter is a fair sample of the women a man can expect to find in Denver City, then I would have done better to stay in St. Louis.*

Cole Estes was a stagecoach man, born and raised with the rumble of heavy wheels in his ears. Because he knew the business, and because he had demonstrated an affinity for a fight on numerous occasions, he was the one to whom Mike Forrest had come. He had known Mike in Illinois five years ago when they had both worked on the Illinois Central and Kansas Territory stageline.

There's a squeeze on me here, Mike had written. **The I. C. & K. T., driven out of business in Illinois by the railroads, have moved their headquarters here and are up to their old tricks of eliminating the competition, which in this case happens to be me. I've got a good deal here, Cole, a mail contract and a chance to run a line from Denver City to the mines on the Vasquez. I've got some pretty good equipment for a small outfit. But I'm too old to put up the fight it's going to take to beat them. There's a quarter interest in it for you, if you want to come, and we whip the big boys.**

A postscriptum at the end of Mike's letter had stated: **My daughter's coming out here, leaving Leavenworth on the 20th of August. I worry some about her, traveling on my line, and I wouldn't let her travel on theirs. Maybe you could time your trip so's you could ride the same coach with her. I'd consider it a big favor, Cole. I'd know she was safe, then.**

So here he was, wet-nurse to a high-and-mighty squirt of a girl, heading into a trouble-shooting job on a line that probably wasn't worth the candle. He shook his head impatiently, still dimly aware of the steady drone of conversation within the stage.

The coach dipped into a cutbank, crossed a wide and nearly dry river bed, turning then to ascend the opposite bank. Turned thus, Cole had a glimpse of another stage, thundering along behind them, and this stage was as different from the one he rode as a Kentucky race horse is different from a shaggy Indian pony.

Under a thick layer of dust its wheels gleamed brilliant yellow. Neither dust nor mud had been able entirely to dull the gleam of its side panels, lustrous varnish that even yet threw

14

back the gleam of the afternoon's brassy sun. A Concord Ox-bow. A new one.

Automatically and without thinking, Cole scanned the road ahead, the road that wound along the precipitous river bank. Knowing all the tricks of stageline war, his thought could only be: *A perfect place for wrecking another coach.*

He shrugged and forced himself to relax against the seatback. Conversation had stopped within the coach, and both Hobart and the woman, who faced the rear, now pulled aside the curtains and craned their necks for a glimpse of the strange coach. Schoonover grumbled: "If I'd known they were this close behind us, I'd have ridden in that coach and been comfortable."

Norah stiffened and started to speak, her bridling anger plain. But Cole interrupted: "I've ridden them, my friend, and there's little difference. They're not made for comfort or intended for it, just to get you where you're going, alive if possible."

Schoonover grumbled unintelligibly. Cole said, his oblique glance on Norah: "I've a notion this lady is related to Mike Forrest who owns this line. Your blamed grumbling is getting her goat."

He became aware of the Concord's lead team drawing abreast, and suddenly the driver's whip popped sharply above their heads. Deeper into the harness they seemed to lunge, and in an instant their increased speed brought the second team into view.

Cole growled: "Devil of a place to pass." Uneasiness was a pressure upon him. His body bunched and tightened involuntarily against the seat, and he remembered his responsibility to Mike who expected him to bring Norah through safely simply by his presence in the coach with her.

A quick glance to his right showed how perilously near the bank were the wheels of the Troy. And then suddenly Cole was on his feet as he felt the front wheel of the Concord touch their own rear wheel. Leaning across Schoonover, he thrust his head from the window. "Pull up, damn you! You want to put us in the river?"

He got no answer, but he heard a laugh, mocking, faint, all but lost in the rumble of wheels, in the thunder of hoofs.

Alarmed thoroughly now, Cole pulled himself back and thrust his head and shoulders through the window on his own side of the coach. Standing on the seat he could just reach the baggage rack atop the coach. Gripping this, he pulled his legs through the window, dangled a moment, and then began the swinging, climbing ascent. He felt the touch of the wheels of the other coach again. He yelled at the driver above him: "Pull left, you crazy fool! Don't let him pass you here!"

The driver, high-cheekboned and slit-eyed as an Indian, threw him a pitying and disgusted glance over his shoulder that said plainly: *I got to drive hosses that ought to be pullin' freight wagons. I got to ride stages like this one. On top of all that I got to listen to a loud-mouthed passenger tell me how to drive.*

These things, Cole knew, he would have said if he had time. Cole's head came up until he could look over the coach at the Concord. In the faces of both driver and guard he could see cold, impersonal confidence, and only then did Cole know surely that their plain intent was to put the Troy over the bank and into the dry river bed.

Crouched atop the swaying pile of freight and baggage, Cole half drew his gun, but stopped as the muzzle of the guard's rifle on the stage opposite swung to cover him. The man, a bearded and red-faced giant, shouted: "Put it up, or I'll blow you clear off of there!" Cole let his hand come reluctantly away.

The driver of the Troy, hunched and intent, drew his horses left, relentlessly, recklessly. Cole felt the Concord's front wheel lock with the Troy's rear wheel and heard Norah Forrest's shrill

16

scream. The driver must have heard it, too, must have suddenly become aware of her, of his responsibility to her because she was Mike Forrest's daughter, for he tightened his reins. Unwillingness, reluctance were in the disgusted shake of his head.

Now, Cole thought, *the Concord would pull clear, knowing a woman was involved.* This must have been the driver's thought as well, for he kept a steady pull against his reins. As the Troy slowed, the Concord moved on, cleared their wheels, then forged steadily alongside. Cole turned sick with the realization that the safety of the woman meant less than nothing to them.

The driver of the Troy seized his whip, and it snaked out across the backs of his teams, popping violently. The horses laid into their traces, but this came too late. The coach was too ponderous, too heavily laden to show a change of speed in the split seconds that were left. Relentlessly the Concord drew alongside until it was fully abreast of the smaller coach. Cole knew the pattern of what would happen now. The driver of the Concord would crowd his horses roughly against those drawing the smaller Troy, forcing them off the bank.

Suddenly rage possessed Cole completely. He seized the whip from its socket beside the driver. It snaked out, but this time it was laid directly across the back of the Concord's guard. The man rose out of his seat, a harsh shout of pain breaking from his lips. His rifle fell into the whirling dust between the two coaches. Cole drew his revolver. The driver turned to yell at him: "Get the lead hoss on the far side!"

The Troy lurched violently. The driver sprawled out across the seat, fighting to hold his reins, fighting for balance. Cole felt the lurch as it started and flung himself down recklessly, and it was only this that saved him from being thrown clear. But in the instant it took him to regain his feet, to raise the Colt again, the Concord's teams were drawn roughly against his own horses, forcing them in a screaming, fighting tangle off

17

the bank, a sheer drop of ten feet.

The coach tilted at an awful angle, and Cole was flung clear, still clutching his revolver. His last consciousness was of a terrible, rending crash as the old Troy toppled into the river bed, of Norah Forrest's terrified scream. Then he struck the hard-baked, sandy clay of the river bed and knew the whirling sickness, the brassy taste of descending unconsciousness. Before full blackness overtook him, he had the hazy remembrance of a flurry of shots, of distant, violent shouting.

II

THE STAGE WON'T BE COMING

Wetness along his whole side brought Cole to his knees, and he found himself in the middle of the thin stream that was all there was to Bijou Creek in the late summer. Not fully comprehending the circumstance that had put him here, he stared about dazedly. He saw the coach, lying on its side, its wheels still spinning. Dust raised by its falling had not yet settled.

He muttered thickly: "Couldn't have been out more'n a minute or two." He struggled to his feet, head throbbing and whirling. A steady, low cursing came from within the coach. Cole climbed to the top side of it and raised the door until it lay open, until he could look down inside. Hobart, the lanky farmer, broke off his steady cursing, and squinted up at Cole. Cole asked, his eyes glued to the still form of Norah Forrest: "You hurt, man?"

Hobart grunted. "Shook up, I think that's all." He struggled to his feet.

Cole lowered himself into the coach and pulled the inert form of Schoonover from across Norah's body. Blood oozed from a gash in Schoonover's forehead.

Now he knelt beside Norah Forrest. She lay tumbled in a heap against the door, utterly still. Hobart asked: "What the devil happened? It looked to me like they deliberately wrecked us."

"They did!" Cole laid his head against Norah's breasts and, as he felt their regular movement, sighed with relief. "Mike would never forgive me if she was hurt," he muttered under his breath.

He gathered her into his arms and stood up, laying her on the top side of the coach while he climbed out. Then he took her up again, carried her to a place shaded from the sun by the bank, and laid her down. Hobart followed him out, limping. "What about Schoonover?" he asked.

"Toss a hatful of water into his face. He'll come out of it."

Hobart limped back toward the coach to look for his hat. Cole tore a strip of lace from Norah's exposed petticoat and went to soak it in the narrow stream. Returning, he stared down at her for a moment. Her dress, revealingly low-cut, had fallen away from her shapely ankles. Her hair, not quite black, was in complete disarray.

Sprawled out this way, her face smudged and dirty, there was an earthiness about this woman that Cole would not have believed possible. Her dress molded each curve of her body faithfully, showed its sensual, virginal beauty. He felt again a strong attraction. He said aloud: "There's nothing much wrong with you that the flat of Mike's hand once in a while wouldn't cure."

He knelt and realized suddenly that a thin film of sweat had dampened his brow. He bathed the dirt carefully from Norah's face. Norah stirred but did not wake. Suddenly, conscious of Hobart's glance, Cole stood up. His voice carried an unwonted hoarseness. "She'll come out of it in a minute," he said, "and then she can tell us for herself where she's hurt. Hanged if I want to poke around, looking for broken bones."

Schoonover sat on the sand beside the coach, looking like a five-year-old who was about to cry. Hobart asked worriedly: "How the devil we going to get to Denver City now?"

"The next station can't be over fifteen miles." Cole rummaged about in the sand until he found his gun. He removed the barrel and poked a scrap of his shirt through it. Reassembling the gun, he walked to the place, fifty feet away, where two of the horses lay, legs broken, in a welter of tangled harness. He placed a shot in the head of each and then came back, reloading the Colt from the powder flask he carried at his belt. "I'll go see if I can catch one of the others in a minute," he told Hobart. "You and Schoonover stay here with her. The Indians aren't hostile, but all this plunder, scattered out on the ground, would be one devil of a temptation."

The shots had brought Norah Forrest back to consciousness. Now she sat up, her eyes dazed and uncomprehending. A quick stab of worry turned Cole's voice unnecessarily rough. "Can you stand up?"

She nodded.

"Do it then. I've got to know if you're hurt before I leave."

For an instant she stared at him. Then stubborn and willful anger stirred in her dark eyes. "Just who do you think you are, anyway? I'm perfectly comfortable right here, and I have no intention of getting up!"

Cole went to her and stood for a moment, looking down. "Last chance," he grinned.

She did not reply. Haughty arrogance grew on her face. Cole reached down and caught her under her arms, bringing her to her feet. The arrogance left her, and her lower lip turned soft and trembling. Cole thought frantically: *Hell, she's going to start crying!* He asked contritely: "You're hurt, aren't you?" He was still holding her.

Wetness grew in the woman's eyes, but she fought this back, glaring. "I am not! I'm perfectly all right!"

Cole said, half smiling: "I think I ought to feel your legs for broken bones."

Norah yanked her hand loose and brought it sharply against his face. Cole laughed, tightening his hold on her. She demanded: "You let me go! Do you hear?" Her small hands beat futilely against his chest.

Cole asked: "Would you like to walk around and show me that your legs aren't broken?"

She nodded, glaring, her lips set in a firm, straight line. Cole released her, his eyes twinkling. Defiantly she flounced around a ten-foot circle. "There! Now are you satisfied?"

"Not entirely, but it's a good start."

Hobart, poking about in the rubble of baggage, suddenly exclaimed: "God! Look at this!"

Cole left the angry woman and went behind the coach. Half buried in baggage and freight lay the driver's body. His head was twisted at an odd angle, and the life was gone from him. A strong odor of whiskey rose from him. Hobart grinned. "Drunk."

Cole said: "He was as sober as you are. That smell is from his bottle. It broke in the fall." He shrugged impatiently. "It's getting late." He strode to the high bank and along it until he came to a place where he could climb out. A quarter mile away he could see the four remaining stage horses, quietly grazing, harness still hanging from them. Along the road toward Denver, though, not more than a hundred yards away, stood a gray horse, saddled and bridled, reins dragging.

Quick surprise touched Cole. He moved in that direction, speaking soothingly to the horse as he approached. When he was but fifty feet away, he fell abruptly silent, for now he could see the man that had ridden this horse.

Recognition stirred in Cole. He broke into a run, and the horse trotted nervously away, head turned so that his feet did not step on the trailing reins.

The man on the ground was short, stockily built, with a mane of shaggy hair, turning gray. One of his eyes had been shot away, and in its place was a horror of red and clotted blood. His other eye was open, staring and vacant. Cole croaked: "Mike, hang it, I told you I'd bring her to Denver all

22

right. Why the devil did you have to come out to meet her?"

Moving again after the horse, he thought: *This is going to be tough on her. If she's got any of Mike in her, it'll come out now. If she hasn't . . . well, we'll see.*

Pushing the gray, Cole reached the stage station about two hours later. It was a hastily thrown up building of rough lumber, having but one large room downstairs, a part of which was curtained off, and a low-ceilinged loft where, Cole supposed, the women passengers slept. What furniture Cole could see was homemade, consisting of a long table, a bench on either side, a couple of packing boxes, and an empty whiskey keg.

Finding no one in the building, Cole came outside again and walked to the corrals where he found the station agent, currying a horse, one of six he had tied to the fence. He said: "You can turn them loose. The stage won't be coming."

"Why not?" Suspicion was in the man's tone which had a dry, nasal twang. Before Cole could answer, the man said sharply: "Who're you?"

The agent was a small man, stooped a little, and very thin. His skin was like brown wrapping paper that had been stretched too tightly over his face and hands and looked as if it might crack at any moment. His eyes, intensely blue, were narrowed and sharp.

Cole said: "Name's Estes. I was coming to Denver to work for Mike Forrest. A big Concord forced us off the bank, ten-fifteen miles back, and wrecked us. Mike got killed. So did the driver. I want a team and wagon to bring in the passengers and their baggage. You might, if you got two wagons, drive one and bring in the freight."

"Well, I'll be damned!" the agent breathed. "That blamed Oxbow went through here not an hour past. Killed Mike, you say? Hell, if I'd knowed that, I'd've blowed the driver an' guard

23

plumb offa the seat!" The agent stuck out his hand. "My name's Castle. Davey Castle. Hardly ever see a lone rider on this road. Cain't blame a man fer bein' a mite suspicious, seein' how scarce riders is around here." He took off his battered felt hat and scratched his bald dome. Thinning hair at his temples was wet with sweat and plastered against his head by the sweatband of his hat.

Cole said patiently: "How many wagons you got?"

"One . . . rickety as the devil. An' a wobble-wheeled buckboard."

"When's the next stage?"

"Day after tomorrow."

"Could a man make it to Denver in the buckboard?"

The agent shrugged. "You'd hafta be lucky."

"We'll try it. You can send the baggage on the next stage."

Davey Castle, Cole discovered as they caught horses and hitched up, was a voluble man. He confided in lowered tones the reason he had left Maine, which was marital difficulties, and he even went into great detail to be sure Cole fully understood the difficulties and sympathized with him. "The wife was one of these big, buxom women," he finished. "Bossy as all get-out. But my gawd, onct a man got her in. . . ."

Cole interrupted: "I can imagine."

Davey laughed slyly. "You got a good imagination then, brother."

Cole climbed to the spring seat of the buckboard. He asked: "This thing belong to Mike?"

"Yeah. Why?"

"Mike must've taken some lessons in the art of lying. He told me he had some pretty good equipment."

Davey doubled up with laughter. He slapped a skinny thigh. "Mike must've exaggerated some," he admitted.

Cole touched the backs of the horses with the reins, saying:

24

"The wagon'll be slower. We'll bring in Mike and the driver. You bring everything else, huh?"

Davey nodded, and Cole drove away.

Full dark blanketed the plains long before Cole Estes drove the buckboard into the station yard. Fatigue had long since silenced the grumbling Schoonover. Norah sat between Cole and Hobart on the spring seat, her face still and white. Behind, with Schoonover, rode the two bodies, wrapped in blankets. As the fat merchant tumbled off behind, Cole asked: "Can you cook?"

"What's the matter with her?"

Hobart grunted: "Go lay down somewhere. I'll do it."

Norah murmured: "I can do that much . . . if one of you would light the lamp for me."

Hobart said: "Sure. You come on in with me." He added over his shoulder to Cole: "I'll be out in a minute. Bring an extra shovel."

Cole drove the team to the corral, unhitched, and turned them loose. Then he rummaged in the lean-to behind the station until he found two shovels whose handles were unbroken. In this inky blackness it was difficult to find a place that might be suitable, viewed by daylight, for a burial ground. Remembering a tiny knoll to the westward, he started his first grave there. Hobart came out shortly and began one beside Cole's.

Cole was two feet down when he heard Norah's call to supper. He and Hobart ate their greasy side meat and potatoes in silence, then hurried back outside. When Davey Castle brought the lumbering, creaky wagon into the yard at midnight, Cole was just finishing, and Hobart was down to his shoulders. Cole said: "Deep enough," and climbed out, sweating.

He sent Hobart after the others. When they came, bringing lanterns and the buckboard with the two bodies in it, Cole said

25

to Hobart: "I never went to many funerals. Do you remember what to say?"

Hobart, apparently a deeply religious man, nodded and said the burial service from memory in his deep, halting voice. Norah Forrest stood tearless and numbed beside him.

Walking back toward the stage station, with discouragement and utter tiredness in his muscles and mind, Cole thought: *You were crazy, Mike. No one could build a heap of junk like you've got into anything but what it is now . . . or worse. I'd do you no favor, or her, either, by trying. So I'll tell her to sell out and go back home, which is what she ought to do.*

With his mind made up, he slept as soon as his long body touched the hard, puncheon floor.

III

DENVER CITY

Across the trickle that was Cherry Creek, Denver City had a lusty air of brawling, uncouth growth. On every hand were the naked skeletons of buildings in the process of erection. From somewhere on Cole's left he could hear the high whine of a sawmill, and over the babble of voices, shouts, and ringing hoofs on hard-packed streets came the incessant chatter of hammers pounding nails, of handsaws, of sledge against iron stake. Perhaps a dozen buildings, being two stories high, stood out above the others. At McGaa Street a new bridge spanned the creek, and at Blake stood another, rickety and tilting in the middle.

From Wazee to the Platte, half hidden by cottonwoods, stretched hundreds of tents, wagons, and lean-to shacks. An Indian village was a sore upon the landscape north of the furthermost of these, and between the Indian village and the town were two wagon trains, drawn into rough circles.

Norah Forrest sat between Cole and Hobart on the spring seat, and the two of them wedged her in and kept her propped upright. Cole asked: "Where are your father's corrals? And where is the stage depot?"

"The stage depot is at the Quincy House. He never mentioned the corrals."

Cole halted the buckboard before a bearded miner near the McGaa Street bridge. The man stared at the buckboard, at its crooked wheels, and said before Cole had a chance to speak: "You didn't come all the way from Leavenworth in that contraption, did you, brother?"

Cole shook his head, a half grin softening the corners of his

27

wide mouth. "Makeshift. Our stage was wrecked. Where's the Quincy House, brother?"

The man spat a stream of tobacco juice into the dust. He grunted: "Two blocks ahead, one to the right. Cain't miss it. It's just around the corner from the Elephant Corral."

Cole drove on and, at the designated corner, turned right. A huge, stable-ringed corral on his right proclaimed itself to be the Elephant Corral, and across Wazee and north a way was another, nearly as large, which was the Gigantic. At the western end of the Gigantic Cole saw a small sign with the letters, **F. O., D. C., & A** carelessly painted on it. Seeing no hotel, Cole swung right again on F Street and halted his team before a cream-colored, false-fronted building over which hung the sign **Quincy House.**

He caught Norah as she slid to the ground. He said: "What you need is about twelve hours of uninterrupted sleep. I'll go over what Mike's got in the meantime, but, if all the rest is like what I've seen so far, I want no part of it and neither do you."

He sorted her baggage out and set it on the boardwalk. Schoonover jumped down off the pile of baggage and shook himself like a fat terrier emerging from water. "I'll be at the Planter's House," he said pompously. "Have my baggage sent there."

Cole muttered dryly: "If you want a change of clothes before tomorrow, take it with you."

Schoonover started to protest, but Cole's steady glance upon him changed his mind. Grumbling, he sorted a bag from the pile and waddled up the street with it clutched in his hand.

Cole followed Norah into the hotel and set her bags down inside the door. Norah was at the desk in conversation with the clerk, a young man who lost no time in making himself agreeable. Cole backed out the door and climbed again to the buckboard seat. "Where you going to stop?" he asked Hobart.

Hobart shrugged. "Leave my stuff in the buckboard. I'll get it later."

The Gigantic Corral, while not so large as the Elephant, nevertheless covered nearly two acres. The corral was formed by open-front sheds on three sides, by two gates and an auctioneer's platform on the fourth. At each of the two corners nearest the gates stood small, enclosed buildings, one of which, Cole guessed, was a tackroom, the other an office. In the exact center of the compound thus formed stood a long watering trough, fed by a hand pump at one end. One of the sheds, fenced off by poles, contained loose, freshly cut hay.

There were buggies and buckboards, wagons and a welter of harness, but there were no coaches inside. Cole said: "Hell, the sign said. . . ."

Hobart pointed. "The sign's down there."

Cole stared. Parked along the western side of the Gigantic were half a dozen Troy coaches, all in a sorry state of disrepair. A corral made of poles, roughly a hundred feet across, contained perhaps twenty horses. Between corral and coaches stood a weathered tent and before this, on a folding stool, sat a bearded man, a short pipe between his teeth.

Cole snorted disgustedly. "If Mike wasn't dead, I'd give him a cussing! I've run across some liars in my time, but Mike tops them all!"

"There's always the mines."

Cole pulled the buckboard toward the tent. Suddenly it hitched and dropped. The horses started, but Cole held them in, cursing. The right rear wheel had come off the buckboard, putting the axle into the dirt. Cole called to the man before the tent: "Come and get it, my friend. It belongs to your brokedown stageline. Set my bags inside your tent, if you will, and I'll be obliged."

Without waiting to see if the man would comply, he jumped

29

down and strode up the street, with Hobart hurrying to catch up.

For a block he walked in silence, fuming. Finally he asked: "Leaving for the mines right now?"

Hobart murmured in his easy drawl, "Ain't in too much of a hurry. A man ought to know where he's going before he leaves. But once he's in the water, he'd ought to swim."

"A sly dig."

"'Twasn't meant so. Could have been this man Forrest needed you so bad, he stretched the truth some. Strikes me that girl's going to need someone to look after her."

"You do it, then. I keep thinking how bad she needs someone to spank her, though I doubt if I could keep my mind on spanking if I ever got her turned across my knee."

Hobart ignored the jest. He paused uncertainly at the intersection, staring up Blake toward the towering and imposing shape of the Planter's House, a block away. "I got me half a notion to pitch in an' give her a hand myself."

Cole stared. Abruptly he laughed. It sounded harsh and caustic. Hobart stiffened angrily.

"If she was horse-faced and bony, would you feel the same way?"

Hobart's muscles bunched, but then he seemed to change his mind. He said: "Don't sneer at a man for the decent things he wants to do. I'm old enough to be that girl's father. I had a girl myself once that would be about her age . . . if she'd lived."

Shame touched Cole, but it did not soften him. "I'm sorry. But there's little chance for anyone, bucking a big line with an outfit like Mike's. I've seen the big lines work too often. Forget that girl and go on to the mines. She's got a mail contract to bargain with. She'll sell out and go back East where she belongs."

30

Hobart toed the dust aimlessly. "Maybe you're right." Together they walked in silence the rest of the distance to the Planter's House.

Night came down across this land, black velvet that began at the jagged peaks and rolled eastward. Lamps winked in windows, and tradesmen laid aside their tools. Working men plodded homeward, and the saloons began to fill. A flurry of shots could be heard in the direction of the McGaa Street bridge, followed by a ragged shout of pain.

Cole stood at his front window in the Planter's House and stared down into the street. A wagon loaded with logs lately arrived from the mountains passed, heading southeastward. Try though he would, Cole could not shake off his uneasy feeling of an obligation unfulfilled. Not more than an hour past he had called at the Quincy House with the thought in him that he would give her his refusal and be done with Mike's whipped and broken stageline once and for all. Norah, however, he was informed, was undoubtedly still sleeping, since no sound had issued from her room all afternoon. So he had left a note, brief but to the point.

Dear Miss Forrest,
Sorry, but I can't see it. Get yourself a lawyer and use your mail contract to bargain with. But sell out. It's the only way you can come out with anything at all.

Cole Estes

He saw a woman approaching along Blake, and even in the semi-darkness there was something about her movements that reminded him of Norah Forrest. He experienced an unwilling feeling of guilt and angrily shook it off. Still watching, he saw

31

her pass through a beam of light that fell across the walk, and relief touched him. *Dance-hall girl* was his thought, for the woman's clothes were quite obviously not the sort Norah Forrest would wear.

He turned from the window. The sight of the dance-hall girl had vaguely stirred him, had made him remember the one remedy always successful in curing him of moodiness, of too much fatigue — liquor and a woman, in that order, for in this as in all frontier towns often a man needed the liquor to make him forget that the woman was hard and coarse and faded.

Moved from his thoughts by vague anticipation, he took off his shirt and splashed vigorously in the tin basin that stood on a table against the wall. Straightening, reaching for the towel, he heard a small, short knock against his door.

"Come in." He walked toward the door, scrubbing his face and chest with the towel. When the knock came again, more strongly, he yanked open the door. His mouth dropped open. For a moment he stared, then humor entered his eyes and touched the corners of his somber mouth. With a towel-wrapped forefinger, he wiped soap from one of his ears.

"I saw you down in the street. I thought it looked like you, but decided it wasn't, when I saw your clothes."

A flush crept up to stain Norah Forrest's too-pale cheeks. She asked: "May I come in?"

Mockery was in Cole's gray eyes. "It's improper for a lady to enter a gentleman's bedroom even in this god-forsaken wilderness. People will talk."

"Oh, stop it! I want to talk to you. I got your note." She came in determinedly but kept her eyes averted from his naked chest and its mat of fine hair. Cole took his shirt from the chair back and slipped it on, deliberately watching her. He asked: "Where the devil did you get that dress?"

32

"I borrowed it from a girl at the Quincy House."

"A dance-hall girl?"

"I didn't ask what her profession was."

"Was it that obvious?" Cole was grinning openly.

Norah stamped a small foot angrily. "I didn't come here to discuss my dress, or a dance-hall girl, either."

"What did you come for?"

For a moment he thought she would leave. Anger sparked dangerously in her deep brown eyes. Her lips, that he remembered could be so soft and inviting, were not so now. Her firm chin was uptilted and very slightly thrust out. Arrogance was plain in her, as was the fact that she wasn't used to opposition and refusal.

With an obvious effort she controlled herself, even managed a tight little smile. "I came to thank you. You were very brave at the time of the wreck, and very considerate afterward."

Cole laughed outright at her obviously rehearsed speech. "And?"

"Oh, stop it! You're insufferable!"

"But you'd like to change my mind?" Deliberately he let his glance drop from her face to the dress, sheer and revealing and tight-fitting, to her tiny waist, flat stomach, full, rounded hips. In spite of himself he felt his pulses quickening, felt a lessening of his amusement.

"Yes, I would. If you are afraid you would not be paid. . . ."

Cole interrupted. "No, I've worked at staging all my life, and I know what can be done and what can't. If you are careful, you can come out of it with several thousand dollars. Then you can go back East."

Norah's small chin set stubbornly. Anger again stirred in her eyes. "I'll do no such thing. D'you hear? I'll not go back beaten. If you were not so. . . ." She paused, making a strong and determined effort to suppress her frustration.

"Cowardly?" Cole supplied, grinning.

"It was the word I had in mind. But, perhaps, I was wrong. Perhaps, you are thinking in terms of money and are waiting for me to make you a better offer than Father did."

"It might be interesting, but it wouldn't make me change my mind."

"Would a half interest in the line . . . provided you win . . . interest you?"

Cole shook his head.

Pure desperation shone for a moment in Norah's eyes, and this was puzzling to Cole. She took a step closer to him, managed a smile, and almost managed a provocative look. She asked softly: "Would I interest you?"

"Not if it comes as hard as all that." With complete suddenness the humor went out of Cole entirely. His hands reached out, caught her by the waist, and drew her roughly against him. His head bent, and his lips caught and held her own parted lips. For an instant she held herself rigid. Then, quite obviously remembering that this had been her own suggestion, she softened, but it was only the softness of acquiescence. Still Cole crushed her against him, his lips bruising and hungry.

All at once Norah's body arched upward against his. Her arms crept around him, and her fingers bit into his neck, the strength of her awakening demand in them. Breathing harshly, Cole pushed her away, his eyes still hot.

Norah searched his face, her expression wondering, and then she murmured, "You will help me, then?"

Cole laughed mirthlessly. "No. The sort of thing you're trying to offer can be bought anywhere in Denver City for much less."

Norah stared at him as though he had struck her. Then, as the blood drained out of her face, her eyes took on a look of untrammelled rage. Surprising him utterly, she sprang at him, and her fists beat against his face. "You . . . ! You . . . !" she screamed, apparently unable to find an epithet strong enough. "I might have known there wasn't a speck of decency in you."

Cole caught and held her arms in a rigid, inflexible grasp. Her helplessness seemed to infuriate her further. "You've used the wrong word," he told her. "What you have suggested does not require decency." The humor of this struck him now. He grinned down at her openly. "I have surprised myself tonight, but you did it so very badly. Now, go on back to the Quincy House and dress yourself like a lady. The first thing you ought to learn is to put the right label on your merchandise."

He had thought she was quite as angry as a woman could get, but now her eyes positively flashed. Reaching the peak of temper, there was possibly nothing left for her but tears. They began in a mistiness over her eyes that deepened until tears welled from their corners.

Suddenly she whirled and fled from the room, slamming the door viciously behind her. Conscious that it was growing late, that this young woman, dressed as she was, might be accosted in the street, Cole reached for his hat. But then he stopped and whirled the hat onto the bed, muttering, "Heaven help the man that bothers her between here and the Quincy House. He'll think he's tied into a bobcat."

IV

TONIGHT I'LL HAVE ALL THREE

Twice during Norah's block-and-a-half walk to the Quincy House a man did approach her, but both times, as Cole predicted, the uncontrolled anger in her stopped them uncertainly before they had more than opened their mouths to speak.

Norah could not remember ever having been so angry. "Oh, I hate that man. I hate him," she repeated to herself over and over again.

But only partly was her anger directed at Cole Estes. Partly it was directed at herself, for she could not forget the way she had responded to his rough and insistent kiss, the way he had pushed her away as soon as he had aroused her. She could forget neither her own words — "Will you help me?" — nor the tender, triumphant way she had spoken them.

Her own honesty was beginning to assert itself by the time she reached her room. She paused before the mirror, gazing with growing distaste at the dress she wore, at her white, full breasts that were more than half exposed. She grew hot at the memory of his words, "Put the right label on your merchandise," and "What you're offering can be bought anywhere in Denver City for less."

He was no gentleman. He was at least not at all like the gentlemen she had encountered at school in the East, whom she easily controlled with an arched eyebrow, a mock frown. Though she did not know it, this experience, or lack of it, explained the youthful arrogance in her that was so irritating to Cole. Raised for the past ten years in an atmosphere where

36

manners were emphasized more than courtesy, where the package was more important than the contents, she was only what they had made of her.

As she slipped out of the dress, she could not shake off the tarnished feeling that came over her. She flung the dress in a heap on the bed. "Damn him! Oh, damn him, anyway!"

"What's the matter, honey? Didn't the dress do the business?" A woman had come into the room, not bothering to knock, and Norah turned with startled surprise.

"Do you know what he said?" Norah asked indignantly.

"What did he say?"

"He said, 'Go back to the hotel and dress like a lady. The first thing you ought to learn is to put the right label on your merchandise.'"

For an instant Norah's visitor stared. Then a smile began at the corners of her mouth, in her weary blue eyes. Suddenly she began to laugh. Tears coursed down her smooth and beautifully translucent cheeks. She gasped: "I'm sorry," and collapsed into a chair, still laughing. "He sounds like quite a man, honey. What's he look like?"

Now, again, anger stirred in Norah, and her face took on an outraged imperiousness. The woman who sat laughing in such an unlady-like position in the big chair was taller than Norah by a full two inches. Instead of Norah's lithe youthfulness, her body had the fullness, the roundness of a woman's body. Her dress was a prototype in shimmering green of the dress Norah had flung on the bed, its purpose being to reveal rather than to conceal the full promise of her body. Her hair, cascading to her shoulders, was a rich, copper red that caught the glow of lamplight and flung back almost metallic glints. "What's he look like?" she repeated.

"Oh, he's tall. He's . . . so darn superior."

The woman, Sally Ambrook, murmured, "A good descrip-

37

tion. I could pick him out of any crowd after that. All men act superior, honey."

"Well, you'll probably see him, fighting, carousing around the place where you. . . ." Norah flushed, then said contritely: "Oh, I'm sorry. I didn't mean. . . ." Sudden awareness came to her of what Sally Ambrook was — a dance-hall girl — a *tarnished lady*.

Sally straightened in her chair and got up. "Nothing to be sorry about, honey. It isn't too bad a life, except your feet get awfully tired."

"Your feet?" Norah's face showed her puzzlement. "I thought. . . ."

"We dance with the customers, honey. That's all." Deep amusement lurked in Sally's eyes, but there was pity there, too, and regret for Norah's sudden and terrible embarrassment. "No wonder he finds it so easy to torment you, you poor kid. Now quit thinking and get to bed. You've had a tough time of it with your father and all. I've got to get to work or get fired."

Norah nodded dumbly, and watched as Sally moved gracefully to the door. When it closed behind her, Norah flung herself face downward on the bed, sobbing. A terrible feeling of loneliness oppressed her, like a leaden weight upon her spirits. This afternoon she had discovered, by a visit to Clark Gruber and Company, her father's bank, the true distress of the stageline's position. Riddled with debt, owning only worn-out equipment, the line had a mere three hundred dollars in the bank, less than enough for one week's operation. Aware fully that her father had sent her money for years at the cost of stripping his business, an awakened sense of loyalty to Mike had sent her to seek out Cole Estes, prepared to offer herself, if need be. Now, even this chance was gone before his coarse refusal.

She got up and blew out the lamp, removing the rest of her

clothes in darkness. Then she flung herself upon the bed, sobbing into the pillow, and so fell asleep. But all through the night she was tortured by the recurring crash of the coach as it tumbled into the dry river bed, by the dreadful sight of her father, whom she had seen not at all for three years, a crumpled and lifeless figure in the dust.

Another figure was also in her dreams, Cole Estes, finding all her weaknesses with uncanny precision, and mocking her for them. Strangely, though, through all this his eyes were full of gentleness.

Denver's finest, the Gold Coin Saloon, was easily distinguishable by its sign, a four-foot reproduction of one of Clark Gruber and Company's privately minted twenty-dollar gold coins, that bore the legend across the top, **Pike's Peak Gold**, and a picture of a rather improbable mountain in the center beneath which were the words **Denver** and **Twenty Dollars**.

The building itself was a towering two-and-a-half story affair, festooned with scrollwork along its eaves and balcony. The tinkle of a piano, freighted from the East at prodigious cost and effort, came through its open doors, rising tinnily above the well-bred murmur of talk and merrymaking.

Cole moved leisurely across the thick-piled carpet and found himself a place at the long, elaborately carved bar between two groups of earnestly conversing men. The talk centered on the gold fields of the Vasquez where, the previous year, Gregory had made his fantastic discovery.

"But what good are these gold fields doing either their discoverers or Denver City?" asked one of the men. "The miners are afraid to work more than enough to pay their bare expenses for fear of robbery. There is never a day passes on the Vasquez, or on the road between here and there, but what one or more men are waylaid and murdered for their gold."

The man beside Cole, a short-bearded, calm, and thoughtful man, replied without heat. "It is eventually going to become our responsibility to see that they have law and protection . . . if not law as we have known it in the East, then a committee of citizens who will track down these criminals and punish them. Surely you agree with that, General Larimer?"

"Then perhaps you will suggest such a possibility in your paper, Mister Byers. I have talked that idea for months up and down the streets of Denver. Everyone agrees that it is necessary, but nobody does anything about it."

Cole brought the flat of his hand down on the bar with a resounding whack. Byers, next to him, started. A bartender, white-aproned and bearded, came toward him. Cole said: "I'm here to drink and not to talk. But I would make a bet that, if I had a claim on the Vasquez, I would work it and heaven help the man who tried to rob me."

Byers said quickly: "You sleep like the dead after a day at a sluice box. And in the dark no man is a match for half a dozen."

Cole shrugged, but he was unconvinced. He poured a drink from the bottle that now sat before him and downed it at a gulp. Anticipation was a fever in him. The odd feeling of tension, that he had felt so often before, was in his head and in the lightness of his muscles. There were things that could ease this tension. Liquor was one. A fight was another. A woman was a third. Cole thought: *Tonight I'll have all three.*

A fiddler joined the piano player, and the two struck up a lively tune. Now the girls came down the stairs, hips swaying, eyes smiling. A murmur of appreciation rose from the crowd. Cole turned his head to watch the girls and felt a touch of surprise, for not one of them was over twenty-five, and, while their eyes were too worldly, none was coarse and none faded. Their white skin gleamed softly in the light from a dozen

40

glittering crystal chandeliers. Quick excitement touched Cole. He poured another drink and tossed it down. The liquor was warm in his stomach, and he felt a loosening of his muscles, coupled with a strong sense of well-being.

A man in the group with Byers and Larimer chortled: "Man, will you look at that redhead!"

Cole looked. This one was tall for a woman, and her hair was a copper red that appeared almost metallic in the soft light. Her eyes were a clear, smiling blue, and her skin was beautifully smooth and almost transparent. She was dressed in clinging, shimmering green that showed the mature roundness of her body. Cole asked: "What's that one's name?"

Byers shrugged. "They are all alike to a man of my age."

Another man in the party snorted. "A man never gets too old for a pretty woman. Her name is Sally Ambrook. But don't get any ideas, my friend, because she dances with the customers, and that's all."

"Then she'll dance with me," Cole murmured, and left the bar. He moved through the crowd and intercepted Sally Ambrook as she came off the bottom step of the stairs. His eyes were friendly, but they also contained boldness and a challenge. "Will you dance this first dance with me?" he asked. "After that, we will see, but I think you'll be dancing several with me tonight."

Her glance ran over him, and her eyes quickened with involuntary interest. Wordless, she laid a soft hand on his arm and moved onto the polished dance floor with him.

Afterward, they found a table, and Cole ordered drinks from a white-jacketed waiter. Sally said: "So you are another of those who have come across the country to take a fortune in gold from the Vasquez?"

Cole shook his head. "I will take a fortune from somewhere, but it will not be from the bed of some stream."

41

Sally's glance was frankly interested. She asked: "How, then?"

Cole shrugged. "I haven't decided yet. Something will occur to me."

"There are too many men already in Denver and on the Vasquez waiting for something to occur to them. Usually what occurs to them is robbery and murder." Her disappointment in him was plain and put him immediately on the defensive.

"I'm not one of those. What is mine is mine, and what belongs to another man is his. Robbery and murder are the tools of cowards."

The waiter brought their drinks, and Cole laid a gold piece on the waiter's tray. As the man made change, Sally observed: "Already I have changed my mind twice about you. I hope I sha'n't have to change it again, because now I find myself liking you."

The waiter moved away, and Sally picked up her drink, set it aside, and then picked up Cole's. "You don't mind? The drinks they serve me are only tea. Tonight I feel the need of something stronger."

She was watching Cole with an odd intentness, as though she were looking for something in him and could not quite decide whether she had seen it or not.

Cole saw her eyes widen, saw her mouth half open to speak. He became aware that her glance had left him and was now fixed on something behind him. The chill of warning traveled down Cole's spine, and he came smoothly out of his chair, moving to one side swiftly as he did so.

Even as he turned, he brought the chair around in front of him. All of this was instinctive in Cole, a defensive action. Now he raised the chair to waist level, a bit startled and moved by half recognition of the man who came at him in such a clumsy rush. The chair leg poked this man in his middle, but he only

42

slapped it aside with a long-reaching arm.

All at once Cole understood. This was the bearded and red-faced guard who had sat atop the Concord Oxbow and across whose back Cole had laid his whip. Cole said, his mouth drawn into a tight grin which had no mirth in it: "I'm glad you found me, my stage-wrecking friend, because I think I owe you something."

Behind the Concord's guard stood a half circle of his cronies, grinning their anticipation, and now one of these said: "Break his arm, Jake. Mess up his face some so Sally won't even want to look at him."

Jake made no effort to hit Cole. He swayed on the balls of his feet, arms hanging at his sides. He was an enormous man, whose chest and belly were one and made him appear top-heavy. His lips showed pink through the inky blackness of his beard. Abruptly and with confusing suddenness Cole moved, striking out with a long-reaching left. Jake's head snapped back, and he took a step backward to retain his balance, but the force of the blow seemed not to affect him at all.

Cole followed with a right, his weight coming forward and all the force of his shoulder behind his fist. Jake's nose flattened and spurted bright blood. But the man only shook his head and swiped at his nose with a sleeve.

This blow threw Cole in close, and he felt the huge paws of his adversary close behind him in the small of his back. He heard a voice: "You got him now, Jake! Break his damned back!"

Cole heard Sally's stifled scream and became aware of the deathly silence that had fallen over the room. Jake's arms, as thick as an ordinary man's legs, tightened inexorably, and Cole felt himself being forced backward. Jake's face was close to his own, the man's breath reeking of whiskey sourness and hot in his nostrils. Jake's lips were grinning, but it was only the grimace

43

of physical exertion and had no humor in it.

Panic touched Cole. He had seen men like Jake work before, and had seen the broken things that were left when the inhuman power of their muscles had done its work. This panic gave him a strength he did not think he possessed, and for an instant he strained with all that was in him against the gradual and inexorable bending of his back. Throwing one last jerk into this effort, he felt himself come straight, his knees break their contact with Jake's. Explosively he brought a leg upward, smashing into the big man's groin, and he felt the fleeting looseness of Jake's grip, even as the grunt of pain broke from the man's lips.

Cole mustered all that was left of his strength and arched his back, twisting at the same time, and throwing his arms between himself and Jake to add further leverage. He felt himself break away and stumbled backward, falling. He rolled, even as he fell, and came smoothly to his knees, cocking his head and squinting upward. He saw Jake diving at him and drove himself upward. He felt the softness of Jake's belly, felt also the man's clutching hands. Cole grunted: "Oh, no! Not again. You won't get your damned hands on me again." He came to his feet, his fists lashing out, driving Jake away from him by their very force and regularity.

He panted: "Every man to his own style of fighting. Now, I'm going to cut you in pieces. I'll wear you down if I can't do anything else."

Again Jake stood, apparently completely relaxed, and his arms were loose and swinging slightly at his sides. Cole leaped in and snapped his head back with a left, following again with his viciously uppercutting right. Jake only stepped back and shook his head. Cole moved in again, darting back after each blow. He thought: *It's like hitting a stone wall. I'll break my hands on him, and I still won't put him down."*

So he put his attention on Jake's eyes, beating at the brows

44

until the blood ran into Jake's eyes, blinding him. Helplessly Jake swiped at his eyes with his sleeve. A voice yelled: "Get your hands on him, Jake! You don't have to see him to break him up!"

Cole was circling, and Jake was stupidly trying to follow his sure-footed and lightning maneuvers. A man said hoarsely: "Quit runnin' from him, you slug! *Fight!*"

This voice came from behind him, and at the same instant he heard Sally's scream, felt the force of two hands on his back, shoving him violently toward Jake. Caught off balance by this unexpected push, he staggered forward, fighting desperately for balance. At the last instant he threw himself aside, but it was too late. He fell against Jake, heard the man's gloating grunt of triumph and felt the awful strength of the enormous hands upon his arm.

Excruciating pain laced along the arm as it bent under the tremendous pressure. Cole felt it crack, and blindness rose before his eyes in nauseous waves. His head was bursting with the pound of blood, of effort. But through his half consciousness he heard a voice: "Drop him, Jake! Damn you, if you want to brawl, do it over at the Criterion! I'll have none of it here."

He was conscious of Jake's release of his arm, of falling. Then, as he fell, Jake's heavy boot swung out viciously, connecting with the side of his head, blotting out entirely all feeling, all consciousness of the indignant murmur of voices that filled the huge room.

V

MEN WILL BE KILLED

As the fight started, Sally Ambrook had half risen from her chair, filled with consternation and with fear for the newcomer. Jake Rupp, in the short time since he had arrived in Denver City, had made a reputation for brutality, and this reputation was built upon the broken bones of lesser men. Realizing then, though, that there was little a woman could do in a thing like this, she sat back again, but tenseness filled her, and she watched with widened eyes and with increasing horror.

The more respectable element in the place moved away from the fight, with no eagerness in them to watch these two beat each other into insensibility, but there was another element that moved in, making a circle about the combatants, eventually shutting off Sally's view. She stood up and became aware of a tall man, elegantly dressed, who now stood before her. This was John Marple, owner of the Gold Coin. He was perhaps forty-five, his sideburns streaked with gray. He wore a short, carefully trimmed beard and a small mustache.

His voice carried no warmth at all as he spoke: "This fight over you, Sally?"

She shook her head. "Jake started it. There was something said about a wrecked stagecoach."

Marple's eyes, never warm, were now exceedingly cold. He muttered: "Damn him! I've warned him." He shouldered his way through the ring of spectators. Sally, following, felt a touch of sickness. Rupp had succeeded in closing with Cole and had the man's arm in the grip of his two big hands. Sally saw the agony on Cole's straining face. She touched Marple's

46

arm. "Stop it! Please stop it!"

"You like this stranger?"

Sally nodded. "Hurry!"

Marple stepped closer to Jake. His hand, flat, came against Jake's bearded face, and his voice, sharp and commanding, snapped the words that Cole had heard.

Jake turned eyes that were somehow clouded and blank toward Marple. Marple repeated sharply: "*Drop him!*"

Jake released Cole's arm, and Cole slumped to the floor. The kick Rupp gave him was a last spiteful gesture of defiance toward Marple. Marple promised: "Some day I'll put a bullet into that stupid head of yours."

Sally looked at Jake Rupp, and an involuntary shudder ran through her. His eyes were nearly closed from the pounding of Cole's fists. His nose was splattered against his face and flattened. The whole front of his beard and shirt was speckled with blood and froth.

Marple's voice, still sharp, said: "Get out of here and don't come back!"

Jake snarled: "I'll kill him!"

"Not in here, you won't, because you won't be in here any more."

For a moment the eyes of the two men locked. Slowly the passion went out of Jake's heavy-featured face. His eyes dropped. "All right," he growled. Marple turned away, facing Sally. His eyes lost some of their hardness, though there was no tangible relaxing of his expression. "Now what?"

Sally heard the music start and felt the thinning of the crowd about her. Again the low rumble of conversation filled the room. Oblivious of her surroundings, Sally said: "He should have a doctor. His arm may be broken."

Resignation showed in Marple's face. He shrugged. "It is one after another, isn't it, Sally? Each one is different, and you think you see what you are looking for in all of them . . . for a time. But it always turns out badly for you. They're weak, or they're cruel, or they're just plain bad. Is there never anything in me for you to want?"

"I can't help myself, John."

"All right. Go get the doctor. I'll have him sent upstairs."

Sally's voice was small and a little ashamed. "I'm sorry, John."

He gave her a twisted grin. "When will you learn that all men are alike? There is good in us all and bad as well. If you find gentleness in a man, you will find weakness with it. If you are looking for strength, you will find cruelty, too. What is it you want, Sally?"

Exasperation touched her because he had found the core of her own uncertainty. She countered with a question of her own: "What do you want, John?"

"You. Just as you are with no changes at all."

"But why me? What is it that you see in me that you cannot see in another woman?"

He shrugged. "I have all the answers except that one, and I won't give you empty flattery because that isn't what you want. I don't know, Sally. What a man sees in the woman he wants is too intangible to explain satisfactorily."

Sally turned, started for the door, but from the corner of her eye she saw a man bending over Cole, gently feeling his arm from which the sleeve had been cut away. She paused, recognizing the man, and went to stand beside him. "Is it broken, Doc?"

He grunted without looking up. "Just got here. Can't tell you yet."

A couple of Marple's waiters hovered a yard away, waiting. Sally asked: "Would it be easier to examine him upstairs?"

"Of course, it would," the doctor said testily.

48

Sally nodded to the waiters, and they stooped, lifting Cole easily. Sally walked beside them, steadying Cole's arm, watching his face all this time. John Marple's words were alive in her memory, and some of the weariness returned to her eyes. She told herself: *You have lived too much and have seen too much. What John says is true. The man you're looking for doesn't exist. You're clinging foolishly to a young girl's dream.* But her eyes, steady and soft on Cole's relaxed face, would not acknowledge her mind's reasoning. After they had laid him down on the silken-covered bed, she continued to watch him while the doctor probed at the arm, and at last she whispered, half trying to convince herself, "It will be different this time. It will be different because he's different."

Cole jerked and sat up. His injured arm came about with a brushing sweep that caught Dr. Fox in his chest and knocked him sprawling on the floor. Fox got up and said irritably: "The fight is over, so you can lay back, and let me finish examining you."

Cole looked at him blankly for a moment, then at Sally, then at the luxuriously furnished room. He made the slightest of grins. "If you weren't here, Doc, I'd think this was heaven. But the angels don't look as grumpy and sour as you do. Is it broken?"

"No. But the muscles are torn, and the elbow's dislocated. I'll put it back in, but you'll do no more fighting for a week and probably longer."

Cole murmured, "All right."

The doctor took hold of his hand and wrist. "It'll hurt. Lay back and brace your feet against the foot of the bed."

Cole groaned. "It hurts now."

"It feels good compared to what it's going to feel like." The doctor put a steady pressure against Cole's wrist. "It's time they ran Jake Rupp out of town. There's hardly a night

49

I don't have to set a bone he's broken."

Anger set Cole's jaw rigidly. "I'll run him out of town, Doc. I'll do that much for you."

Fox snorted and laid back against the pull of Cole's arm. A long sigh escaped Cole's lips, and the muscles of his face strained and twisted.

Sally snatched his free hand in both of hers and buried her face against them. She heard Dr. Fox's brusque: "There. Give it a chance to heal before you go looking for Rupp again, will you?"

Cole's voice was unnatural. "All right."

Sally heard the door close, but she did not raise her head.

Cole said: "This hasn't been the evening I planned for us."

Sally brought up her glance, and there was a mistiness across her vision. She took her hands from his and rose. Cole swung his feet over the side of the bed and sat up. Sally came back with a woolen shawl and made a sling for his arm. Stooping to tie it, her flaming, fragrant hair brushed across Cole's face. She stepped back. "Now."

Cole stood up unsteadily, and this movement put him close to her, his face inches from hers. Sally felt a trembling expectancy, an almost girlish excitement. Her eyes showed some of this youthfulness, this wonder, this pleading, as she looked into his.

Cole's good arm went around her and drew her against him. Sally gasped: "Your arm . . . ?" She did not draw away. His head came down, and his lips found hers, which were soft and warmly eager. Molten fire ran in Sally's veins, and she rose on tiptoes, pressing herself against him. Again conscious of his injury, she drew back and whispered, "Your arm. I don't want you to hurt your arm."

"The devil with my arm!" Cole's voice was hoarse.

Sally smiled. Her soft hands went up and cupped his hard

50

jaw. "Be careful when you leave," she pleaded. "I don't want you hurt again." She could see the cooling of his eyes, and her heart cried out: *I want you to stay! Oh, I want you to stay, but can't you see? You mustn't think I'm like the others, or you won't come back.* She inquired: "I'll see you again?"

He smiled at her, and the smile took from his face all of its somber moodiness, making it pleasant and warm. "You will. Of course, you will. And . . . thank you." He looked at her for a moment more, then turned, and opened the door. Sally watched his broad back from the doorway until he had turned around a bend in the stairway and disappeared from her view.

Now a deep depression settled over her. She thought: *He's not like the others, and he won't come back.* Some inner knowledge told her — *You can't hold a man by holding yourself away from him* — but she argued this fiercely and said softly aloud, "If I were easy for him, he would wonder if I were not easy for every other man as well."

Never yet had Sally given herself to any man, but tonight she would have given herself eagerly to Cole Estes. The thought kept running through her head: *He must be the one, because never before have I felt this way.* Deeply disturbed, she brushed her hair before going down the heavily carpeted stairs again.

Without pausing, Cole went through the crowded Gold Coin and into the crispness of this August evening. The shawl in which Sally had slung his arm exuded a faint fragrance that stirred his senses and brought her likeness vividly before his mind. With his free hand — his right — he fished in his pocket for tobacco, but, realizing that he could not use it one-handed, he tossed it disgustedly into the street. Anger began to stir in him, anger that increased as he thought of the fight. He stopped at a tobacco shop and bought half a dozen cigars, lighting one awkwardly in the doorway of the shop.

Then he continued northeastward along Blake. Reaching

51

the corner of F and Blake, he paused, puffing moodily on the cigar and staring downstreet at the cream front of the Quincy House. A tall, clumsily moving figure approached him from that direction and presently Cole recognized the man as Hobart. He was hurrying, but, when he saw Cole, he halted abruptly. "I've been looking for you!" he panted.

"Why?"

"It's Norah Forrest. Some lawyer's down there, trying to talk her into selling the stageline. I thought. . . ."

"You thought I'd talk her out of it. Well, I won't."

"You were a friend of her father's. You ought to go down there . . . at least help her to get the best kind of deal she can."

Cole shrugged. "All right. I'll do that much. No use in letting them steal it from her."

He walked in the direction of the Quincy House, forced to hurry to keep up with Hobart. Hobart told him jerkily: "I took on a job, working for her, but I doubt if I'll do her much good. I'm a farmer."

Cole felt a touch of obscure anger. "You'll do her no good at all. Why couldn't you keep your blamed . . . ?" He closed his mouth and lifted his shoulders resignedly. *Babes in the woods*, he thought. *They'll be broke in a month if they try to stay in this business.*

There was a small office in the lobby of the Quincy House, situated between the desk and the outer wall. The door stood ajar, and it was toward this door that Hobart led him. As they entered, a man rose, graying, slim, a short man, whose smile contained the professional unctuousness of an undertaker. He smiled and nearly managed to cover the fact that he was irritated. "Ah, Mister Hobart," he said, and, looking at Cole, "I expect you are Mister Estes. Miss Forrest spoke of you as having been a friend of her father's."

Cole took the lawyer's hand. Norah stared at Cole's injured

arm, plainly thinking: *So you have been brawling?* She explained: "Mister Thurston is representing the Illinois Central and Kansas Territory and wants to buy out father's stageline."

Thurston raised a hand, palm outward. "Pardon me, Miss Forrest. Not the stageline. Only the mail contract . . . and the franchise between Denver City and Leavenworth."

Suddenly Norah rose. Her face was white. Cole could see the weariness in her, but her chin was firm and her glance steady. "No. My answer is no. You couldn't even wait until my father's body was cold before you started your grab for what had been his, could you? Do you know that the people who hired you murdered my father and tried to murder me?"

Thurston's face assumed the expression one uses with an erring child. "An accident, Miss Forrest."

Norah clenched her fists. "We'll see what the authorities have to say about that."

"There are no authorities."

"But they shot my father!"

"Did you see it happen? There are Indians on the plains, Miss Forrest. It must have been the Indians."

Cole felt a stir of pity for Norah, so overmatched in this contest. But Norah had not finished. She cried: "Get out of here! Tell them I'll go broke before I sell to them! Father sent me money for years . . . money he could not afford. He stripped his business so that I could have everything I wanted. I didn't know it, then. I know it now. Do you think I'd sell out his life's blood to the same murderers who killed him?" Her voice rose in pitch.

Pure admiration sent a tingle down Cole's spine. He caught Thurston by a skinny elbow. "You hear all right, don't you, friend? She said git."

Thurston snatched up his bag and scurried angrily out the door. Cole breathed, "You sure know how to say no. There's

53

little doubt in him about that."

He turned his glance to her, but the magnificence that had been in her a moment ago was gone. She sank back into her chair, and there was hopelessness in the sag of her shoulders. She put her head down into her hands. "What am I going to do?"

Hobart made a step toward her, but Cole said: "Wait a minute." He was thinking of the words in Mike's letter — "a chance to start a line to the Vasquez" — and he was thinking, too, of the conversation he had overheard in the Gold Coin earlier that evening. Up to now he had seen no hope for Mike's stageline, but coupling the two things in his mind had started a whole new train of thought. He continued: "Miss Forrest, if I were to take on the job of trying to pull this stageline out of the hole it's in, would you back me up, or would you buck me all the time?"

She looked up. Tears blurred her eyes, but she wasn't crying. There was sudden hope in her eyes that made Cole feel ashamed. She stated: "You could do it your way."

"All right. I'll see if you mean that. Tomorrow I'm going to the I. C. and K. T. and tell them you've changed your mind. What did they offer you?"

Norah hesitated, seemed about to protest, but then said: "Three thousand."

"I'd hold out for five." He watched her closely for a moment. Surprise touched his tone as he asked: "You're not going to give me an argument about this?"

Wordlessly she shook her head. Again admiration stirred in Cole. "Then I'll tell you what I've got in mind. At present there's no stage running between here and the Vasquez. The miners are afraid to work their claims more than enough to pay their bare expenses for fear of robbery and because there is no way for them to send their gold to Denver. Your present run between here and Leavenworth is going to have to be given up anyway, because you can't hold it without thousands to throw into its defense. They'll drive you clean out in a month if they put their minds to it."

"Then why do they offer to buy at all?"

"Because, if they force you out, there might be a stink. You could go to the Kansas Legislature, who granted the franchise, and you could go to the Post Office Department, who gave you the mail contract. They figure that three thousand is a pretty small amount to get you out without a squawk, and it is. If the franchise and contract aren't worth ten thousand, they aren't worth a dime." He waited a moment for her to speak and, when she didn't, went on: "Five thousand will give you something to work on for a while. It'll buy men to ride guard on the Vasquez run. And more than that, it will be making them pay for something you know you have to give up anyway."

Hobart interjected: "But is there enough money in a short run like that to make it pay?"

Cole grinned at him. "If you had a claim you could take a hundred dollars a day out of, but you know the chances were at least even you'd be killed for it before you could send it out, how much would you pay to get it safely to Denver? Five percent? Ten? Twenty-five?"

Hobart whistled. "Plenty."

"So will they. We'll charge them ten percent. We'll show the toughs we can be tougher than they are. And we'll be fighting the I. C. and K. T. with their own money because, when they see what we're doing with the Vasquez run, they'll sure as hell want to horn in."

Norah sat upright, her eyes sparkling. In this moment her arrogance was entirely gone. The way she looked at Cole, the way life returned to her, gave him a warm feeling of strength and confidence, but experience had taught him that no venture, particularly one in which your antagonists were strong and well organized, was easy. He cautioned: "It's dangerous. Men will be killed. But . . . it just might work."

Then Norah came across the room and put a hand on Cole's arm. She said: "I've made up my mind. I will sell and go back East. There is nothing important enough to me to have men killed for it, and I know father would have felt the same."

Cole said: "Every day, or nearly every day, some miner on the Vasquez is murdered for his gold. Nothing worthwhile is ever done by evading a fight. If the miners stop carrying gold themselves, the toughs will let them alone and concentrate on us. But there's a difference. We'll be ready and a match for them."

Hobart added his assurances to Cole's, and at last Norah was convinced. Cole put his hand on the door. He said: "Good night" and went out. His mind was busy with the riddle that was Norah Forrest. He had seen only her shallowness at first, but now he was beginning to see other things as well, things that come out only under the pressure of adversity. He thought: *Mike would have been proud of her tonight.*

VI

THE CITIZENS' COMMITTEE

A dozen miles west of Denver City, lying between the long, ridged hogback and the hills that marched away toward the divide, stood a new building called the Mount Vernon House. Built of native, cream-colored sandstone, it served as post office, roadhouse, general store, and saloon, and lay beside the Ute Trail, where it entered the dark, winding Apex Cañon on its way to the Vasquez. Lamps winked from its windows as Fritz Woerner and Edgar Pense mounted their horses at the corral. Fritz yanked his cinch tight with unnecessary violence. "Gott damn it, Ed, I tell you it's shorter if you go south an' break through Hog Back Mountain there."

Ed Pense shrugged. "All right. You go that way. I'll go the other. I'll bet you a bottle of the best rot in Denver that I beat you in. Mind you, though, if your hoss is sweated up, the bet's off. I'll meet you at the Gold Coin."

Fritz Woerner swung into his saddle. "It's a bet." He was a short man, roundly built without being fat. The hairs of his beard were stiff and stood straight out, giving him a look of almost ludicrous fierceness. His eyes were a pale, washed-out blue. He swung away at a trot, heading south. There was no road here, just the tall grass that swished against his horse's legs. The deeply bright stars above afforded only a small amount of light, and Fritz let the deep-chested bay pick his own trail.

Disgust with this country was a thing deeply rooted in Fritz Woerner. Full of hope early this spring he had come West with the rush and had since tramped the Vasquez, Chicago Creek, and had even crossed the vast expanse of South Park. He'd found, where there was gold, all of the claims taken. Elsewhere he found no gold. Finally, broke, he went to work as a miner for day wages that hardly paid more than his expenses. But out of this, he had saved enough for the bay horse and enough for slim provisions along the tedious ride back home.

Now the land began a long, steep slope, and after another thirty minutes Fritz came to a rushing, turbulent stream where it broke through a monstrous gap in the long, seemingly endless ridge called Hog Back Mountain. Here the way was narrow between the steepness of rocky ridge and roily water. And here it was darker. Suddenly a shot blossomed in the blackness ahead, and a voice rang out, thickly accented and touched with madness. "Get back, you murderin' thieves! Followed me, did you? Well, you got it all, and there's none left!"

Fritz reined about frantically in this pitch dark. The voice faded into mumbling nothingness, and there were no more shots. Behind a jutting shoulder of yellow limestone, Fritz paused, thinking: *If I go back and take the other way, Ed'll beat me in, and it'll cost me the price of a bottle.* He squinted up at the rocky steepness of Hog Back Mountain and muttered, "A full half hour it vill take to climb over that." Experimentally he shouted: "I dunno who you are, friend, but I vant nothing you haff. I'm travelin' this way because of a bet that it's shorter than the other, and you delaying me iss going to cost me the price of a bottle."

He got no answer. An odd tingle, partly fear, partly superstition, traveled down his spine. He began to wonder if this had not been imagination. Trembling, but determinedly, he reined his horse again into the defile. Its hoofs rang loudly against the crumbling rock along the trail. Twice in a hundred yards, panic almost controlled Fritz, and both times he reined the horse to a halt but did not turn around. At last, he came out onto the plain, and it was here, in brighter starlight, that he saw the horse, a dim shape against the relative lightness of the plain.

The animal appeared to drowse, not bothering to graze, but, as he neared, Fritz could see that he was saddled, could see his reins trailing. Very tempted to spur out onto the plain, Fritz controlled himself and called cautiously: "Man, are you hurt? Do you need help?"

His voice, unnaturally loud, echoed back from the walls of the defile, from the sheer steepness of the ridge across the creek. But Fritz got no answer.

He rode to the drowsing horse, and the animal lifted its head, staring at him without interest. Close like this Fritz could see all the evidences of hard riding on the animal, from the dried sweat foam that covered him to the utter weariness that kept him rooted to this spot, uninterested even in the lush, drying grass that surrounded him.

Fritz thought, remembering the strange words: *Now, what would I do was I being chased and rode through here?* Looking back toward the defile, he saw a huge rock that had broken from the rim ages past and rolled to the bottom. He murmured, "I'd git me behind that rock."

Dismounting, he advanced cautiously. But not until he was a scant ten feet from the rock did he see the elongated, prone shape of a man behind it. He called, softly, but with the hoarseness of his fear: "Now, don't start shootin', mister. If you'd like to get to Denver City, I reckon I kin help you."

No movement stirred the man. Fritz advanced farther and, at last, could kick the rifle that lay beside the man out of his reach. Then he breathed a little easier. He knelt and turned the man over. Becoming bold, he struck a match and cupped its flickering flame above the stranger's face.

Blood ran from the three-inch gash along the man's temple and had dried and clotted in his beard. His lips were a swollen, purpled pulp, and one of his eyes was completely swelled shut.

Feeling a stickiness on his hand, Fritz examined it, found it covered with thickened blood. He struck another match, held it higher, and found the stranger's right sleeve red and thoroughly soaked. Now Fritz dropped his head and laid an ear against the man's chest. A slow, steady heartbeat brought him instantly to his feet. He said aloud: "You'll bleed to death if that ain't stopped. I'll need a fire to see by. Wonder if they're still after you, or if you got away?"

Taking his chance, he kindled a fire from dead and dry twigs he gathered. Then he cut away the unconscious man's sleeve with his knife. A bullet had smashed the bone, had torn a two-inch ragged hole when it came out. But the bullet had missed, miraculously, any arteries. Fritz tore strips from a blanket he found tied behind the man's saddle and bound them about the arm. Then he led the stranger's horse over. He hoisted the limp body into the saddle, tying his feet and uninjured arm beneath the animal's belly and the man's belt to the saddle horn.

Holding the reins of the led horse in his hand, he mounted and set out across the rolling plain toward Denver City. He should, perhaps, have been thinking of this life he had saved. Instead, he was thinking with characteristic thriftiness: *I'll tell Ed the bet is off. By gott, he can't hold me to it.* But there was no conviction in him. Ed would say, grinning wickedly: *Pay up. I got here first, didn't I?*

John Marple was irritated when they brought the bleeding, dirty miner into the Gold Coin. But, quickly seeing that perhaps this would afford a chance to unify sentiment in Denver City behind a vigilante movement, he ordered two tables brought together and had the man laid there, while the grumbling doctor, roused from his bed, worked feverishly over him.

Standing in the forefront of the circle about the makeshift

operating table, John Marple, tall and without emotion, asked: "Anybody know him?"

He looked closely at the man on the table. The stranger was tall, nearly as tall as John himself. Bearded and badly beaten, there was still a certain handsomeness to his craggy features. The throng stirred, and a voice, far behind him, said: "Let me through. Let me look at him."

John turned and saw a perspiring, clean-shaven fat man, trying to force his way through the crowd. He called again: "Let me through."

As the fat man came out of the press of bodies, Marple asked: "Know him, friend?"

The fat man approached to the doctor's shoulder and looked down. Then he turned. "You are blamed right I know him. I should know him. I played with him as a boy in the old country. His twelve-year-old son is up in my hotel room right now."

Marple asked: "Who is he?"

Apparently not hearing, the fat man asked indignantly: "What kind of a country is this, anyway? George Osten is an honest, hard-working man. He had a claim on the Vasquez that he's been putting fifteen hours a day to working. You want to know why? Because his family is still in Luxembourg. He has not seen them for five years, and George Osten is a man who loves his family. All that five years he has worked, he and the boy, trying to make enough money to send for them, the wife and the other four children. But it is no good. He does not speak English too good and can only take jobs that pay him a little bit. His wife gets sick and cannot work, and the money he sends back goes for food. Then comes the gold rush. George tells me . . . 'It is chance to make enough to send for them,' and he made enough. He had it when he started for Denver. But he does not have it now."

A low growl arose from the packed crowd. The fat man, red

of face and perspiring freely, shouted: "Somebody else have it now. Somebody maybe right here in this room." He stabbed an accusing finger at random. "Maybe you. Maybe you."

The men he had singled out flushed and started forward, but John Marple put himself in their way. He said: "He's naming no names. He's trying to tell you that we ourselves don't even know the men who are robbing us."

A voice from the crowd called: "Then let's find out. Let's find out and string 'em up!"

John opened his mouth to speak but halted as he felt a light touch on his arm. The doctor, gruff and sour, whispered, "No use in me stayin' any longer. He's dead."

Marple said: "All right, Doc." He raised his voice. "Doctor Fox says the man is dead. We've been talking law for a long time now. Are we going to keep talking, or are we going to do something?"

It started as a murmur that swelled in seconds to a roar. Marple raised a hand. "I am not proposing mob rule. That is worse than no law at all. What I am proposing is that a committee of citizens be formed, citizens about whom there is no doubt whatever. When a crime is committed, they, or a posse selected by them, will ride until they catch the culprits. A trial will be held. The guilty will be executed. The innocent will go free."

"I'm for it, John," someone said.

"Me, too," said another. "Let's git busy."

The fat man made himself heard above the uproar, climbing clumsily onto a chair. "That will not help him," he shouted indignantly. "What am I to tell his boy?"

John caught the man's arm and pulled him down. He said: "Osten will be avenged. If it is possible, his son will have his money." Again he raised his voice, and it carried the length and breadth of the room. "Drinks are on the house. While you're drinking, talk over your selections for the members of the citizens' committee. Then we'll vote. Where's the man that brought Osten in?"

He saw the short, round man with the bristling beard and pale blue eyes coming out of the throng. With the feel of his success strong within him, John Marple could still think: *It is a good thing, this law by the people. But for a while it will be overzealous, and the innocent will suffer with the guilty.* He asked: "Where did you find this man?"

"South of the Mount Vernon House vhere the creek breaks through Hog Back Mountain."

"Then we'll send out a posse in the morning with an Indian tracker. If anyone knows anything that might help, it is his duty to report it. We will let these toughs know that it will be harder from now on."

He glanced up and saw Sally Ambrook on the balcony. She was watching him in an odd way that made him feel self-conscious. He dropped his glance and moved out of the crowd and about his business. He had lighted the fire. It would burn now, without him.

VII

RIDE OUT, STRANGER!

Cole Estes walked into the offices of the I. C. & K. T. Express at eight in the morning. A graying, sharp-featured man with spectacles came toward him from behind a long counter. Cole said: "Jess Dyer still run this outfit?"

The clerk nodded.

Cole asked: "Is he here yet?" When the clerk again nodded, Cole said: "Tell him Cole Estes is here."

The clerk shuffled to a door on the far side of the room, stuck his head inside, and mumbled something unintelligible. Then he turned. "He says to come on in."

Cole went into the inner office and closed the door. A man rose from behind a desk — a man grown fat with success — and gave him a genial smile, waving him toward a chair with his cigar. Cole noticed today, as he had often noticed before, that Jess Dyer's smile was a mere habitual contortion of his facial muscles. His eyes remained as cold and hard as polished quartz.

Dyer boomed: "Cole, blame your eyes, what you doin' 'way out here? Haven't seen you for years . . . not since, let's see . . . 'Fifty-Six, wasn't it?"

Cole nodded. "You haven't changed, Jess. It looks like you'd let a man like Mike Forrest alone, seeing as he worked for you for nearly fifteen years."

Dyer guffawed. "Business, my boy. Business. Never let the opposition get their breath."

"Did you know your toughs murdered him?"

The smile left Dyer's face. "Don't get smart with me, boy."

64

Cole shrugged. After a moment he said: "I came out here to give Mike a hand, but you beat me to him. Now his daughter's here, as you know. Last night she turned down your offer for her franchise and mail contract. I talked her into accepting it."

The geniality — the surface geniality — returned to Jess Dyer. "Fine. Fine, my boy. You won't regret it."

Cole finished: "At a slightly altered figure." He let his eyes rest deliberately on Dyer's and they were cool and penetrating and contained a certain challenge.

The smile left Dyer's face. His eyes turned shrewd. He asked: "What figure?"

"Five thousand."

Dyer appeared to consider. "And she'll leave the country?"

"She likes it here. Are you afraid she'll hang Mike's killing on you?"

"I told you once not to get smart with me, Cole. Remember it."

Cole felt his anger stirring. He said: "I've got a few thousand saved. I'm stubborn enough and mean enough to throw it into her line and take a whack at beating you."

"I'll break you."

"Sure. But it'll cost you a hell of a lot more than five thousand to do it."

Dyer shrugged and smiled reluctantly. "All right. You win. Five thousand it is." He went to the door, shouted: "Childs. Bring in those contracts . . . and five thousand in cash."

Cole said softly: "Gold."

Dyer yanked his head around and scowled. "You drive a damned hard bargain." But he shouted into the outer room: "Gold."

Cole said: "Miss Forrest is waiting in the lobby. I'll get her."

"Damned sure of yourself, weren't you?"

Cole nodded.

Dyer stared for a moment, and then he laughed. "How'd you like to work for me again?"

"Isn't Jake Rupp tough enough for you?"

Jess Dyer snorted and for the first time seemed to notice Cole's injured arm. Looking at it, he said: "Tough enough, but not smart enough. Go get this girl, Cole, and when we've finished with her, we'll talk."

Cole brought Norah Forrest into the office with a final caution: "Take his money, sign the contracts, and let it go at that."

Jess handed over the contracts and a heavy small canvas sack of gold coin. While Norah signed the contracts, Cole counted the money. Then he leaned back in his chair. Norah was reading the contracts, and she turned to him with a puzzled air. "It says we must abandon the run between Denver City and Leavenworth, but . . . ?"

Cole said quickly: "That part's all right. They're buying the franchise."

He took the contracts from her and read them through. Satisfied, he said: "They're all right. Wait for me in the lobby and we'll go over to the bank with the money."

Norah gave him a sober glance, then signed the contracts, and went out silently. Cole closed the door behind her. "What did you want to say to me?"

"About that job . . . ?"

Cole interrupted. "Jess, now that I've got the money for Mike's girl, I'm going to tell you something. I liked Mike Forrest, and I like his girl. I have never liked you, and I don't like monopoly. You're going to pay for killing Mike. I'm going to see that you do pay for it."

The full hardness of Jess Dyer's character manifested itself.

His eyes narrowed until they were mere glittering slits. He chewed his cigar for a moment and stared hard at Cole. Finally he said softly: "You've pulled a fast one, haven't you, boy? You've got me to pay for something you were going to have to abandon anyway." He blew a cloud of smoke into Cole's face. "Get out of the country, Cole. Get out while you're still alive."

Cole beat down the anger that boiled in his head. He rose. "You've played at being God for so long you think you are God. You order a man killed, and he gets killed. But you're only a man, Dyer. You can die as easily as any other man. Remember that."

He lifted the sack of gold from the desk. Before he went out, he spoke again. "This is a new country, where every man has an equal chance. There are no entrenched interests, no monopolies. There are a lot of men, like myself, who will fight to see that none get established. Keep Jake Rupp off my neck, Dyer, or you'll be looking for a new bully boy."

He closed the door behind him and stepped out through a side door into the lobby of the Planter's House. Norah Forrest rose and came toward him. The anger on his face seemed to give her reassurance. Cole asked: "Doubting?"

She dropped her eyes. "A little."

Cole said: "He offered me a job."

Arrogance flickered across Norah's face. She began: "Of course, if you. . . ."

Cole interrupted, grinning wickedly: "You going to fire me already?"

"No, but. . . ."

Again Cole interrupted: "I made my decision last night. I didn't want to start a fight that was useless, that there was no chance of winning. There is a chance of winning this one. But you'll need more faith in me than you've got now, because I'm going to do some things you won't like."

For half a block she walked beside him in silence. Finally she asked, her tone rising: "Why can't people let each other alone? Why does there always have to be fighting and killing?"

Cole shrugged, having no ready answer for this. But he said: "There will be a sort of law here before too long. Vigilante law."

"And that will mean more killing."

"It will. It may mean the deaths of men who are innocent. But there is one failing found in law, as you and I know it that is not found in vigilante law. It does not discriminate against a man because he has no money or no influence. It does not favor the rich."

They came to the bank, and Cole followed Norah inside, introduced her, and waited while she deposited the money to the stageline's account. At the door he left her, saying: "I will have to ride to the mines and persuade the miners that we can bring their gold safely to Denver."

Norah asked: "Can we?"

"Maybe. If we can't, you will go back East broke, and I will be on the run from the vigilantes. But, if that happens, at least the miners will be no worse off than they are now."

He left her then, looking somewhat bewildered. An auction was in progress at the Elephant Corral, and Cole bought himself a horse, paying a shocking price but getting a good animal, a long-legged, deep-chested gray, whose mouth said he was five years old. Saddle and bridle for the horse cost him about a fourth of what the horse cost. Satisfied, he crossed Cherry Creek at Blake, turning toward the mountains.

While it was not at all necessary, he rode the ferry across the Platte and paid his toll cheerfully, meanwhile making the acquaintance of the ferryman, a huge, bearded man named Rostov. With the exception of this ferry the road was free then, the ten miles to Golden City, and thence south to the mouth of Apex Cañon where the toll road began.

Cole had his dinner at the Mount Vernon House, so named because of the proprietor's inordinate admiration for George Washington. Then, paying his toll of ten cents for the distance between Mount Vernon House and Elk Park, he set out, alternately walking and trotting the gray.

The way was steep here, and Cole was thankful for the care and time he had used in selecting the horse, for the gray took Cole's crowding on this grade without undue heavy breathing or sweating. This was a land of towering yellow pine, of belly-deep grass, of sheer granite cañon. Aspen thickets made light green patches against the deeper green of the pines. The road kept rising, and at four Cole reached Elk Park, continuing westward to Cresswell, a way station, post office, and saloon.

Leaving, he again paid a toll for the shorter distance between here and the Vasquez, and at dusk dropped down the steep grade into the deep cañon of the Vasquez.

Along this stream winked tiny flares, those of the miners. Cole rode along the road in darkness, coming at last to a fire where half a dozen men hunkered, eating beans from tin plates. He dismounted and approached.

Suspicion brought these men around, facing him, forming a solid wall of hostility. They were all bearded, all ragged and dirty, and reminded Cole more of wild animals than of men. One asked roughly: "What you want?"

Cole felt at a distinct disadvantage. He said: "Name's Cole Estes. I'm starting a stageline from here to Denver City to haul gold mostly. I'm hiring guards and booking shipments."

The hostility in these men was unchanged, but one of them asked: "You guarantee delivery?"

This was the crux of the whole matter, Cole knew. He asked a question of his own by way of reply. "When you ship gold from Denver to New York, does the line guarantee delivery?"

A man growled: "Ain't interested. Ride out, stranger."

Cole turned, bitter discouragement touching him. But a new voice said: "Wait, Joe. This could be a good thing for us all."

Cole swung back and looked at the speaker in the flickering light from the fire between them. He was a tall man and very thin. Not a whit cleaner or less ragged than the others, he nevertheless showed an intelligence not apparent in the others, and his speech was that of a man of education.

Cole said: "No stageline goes further than to guarantee that due care will be used in protecting shipments. And no stageline's guarantee is better than the men behind it. I could promise a guarantee, but, if a large shipment were lost and the line liquidated, there would still not be enough to replace the loss. I'm offering you something better than what you've got . . . which is nothing at all. Not a one of you can sleep soundly. Not a one of you but what is afraid to take your gold and start for Denver. And when one of you does take the chance, he is risking not only his gold but his life as well."

The tall man said: "We'll talk about it." His voice had an air of finality. Again Cole turned. He mounted his horse, continuing downstream. He could feel the unwinking stare of the six against his back and thought: *There's nothing in this world that's worth living in a cave like an animal and fearing all other men until it becomes an obsession.*

He was almost clear of the circle of firelight when an odd feeling of uneasiness possessed him. He almost yanked his head around to look back, but then he thought: *It's only something that I've caught from them. There's so much fear in them that some of it's rubbed off on me.*

He rode another ten feet with the uneasiness increasing until it was a plain tingle in his spine. Not used to ignoring these signs, these hunches, Cole suddenly reined his horse to one side, driving the spurs deep into the animal's sides. Behind him, flame blossomed from the muzzle of a rifle, the racket of the

70

shot reaching his ears an instant later. A smashing blow drove itself against Cole's shoulder, catapulting him from the saddle. He heard the shouting of the men that had been at the fire and then the drumming of a galloping horse's hoofs against the ground.

Not understanding, he drew his revolver, muffling the click of the hammer as he drew it back by holding it between his arm and body. His left shoulder was numb, sticky and warm with the free-flowing blood. Cole heard the voice of the tall miner: "Looks like they didn't want him freighting our gold. And it's too late for us to change our minds now."

Cole called: "Not too late. The light was bad for shooting, and he only got my shoulder."

He got to his knees, still feeling little pain from the shoulder wound, still aware of the numbness in it. He caught his horse and walked toward the approaching men. As his arm swung at his side, the pain came in waves to the shoulder, making these men blur and swim before his eyes. The tall man caught his good arm, steadying him, and led him to the fire. Cole sat down, with no strength left in him at all, and the tall man cut away his sleeve with a knife. After that, there was the searing heat of red-hot iron against his shoulder, which, mercifully, he could stand for only an instant. But through this all he had the feeling that hostility had gone from this group. He heard Joe's ragged voice, just as he lapsed into unconsciousness: "If they want him dead so bad, Vance, mebbe we should want him alive."

Cole awoke once during the night, wrapped in blankets beside the dying fire. For a long while he lay there, staring at the bright, star-studded sky and listening to the steady roar of the Vasquez as it tumbled through the cañon toward the plain below. He dozed then, and, when he awoke again, it was full daylight and nearly a score of men stood around him, looking down. Cole stumbled awkwardly to his feet.

The tall one, Vance Daugherty, said: "We've talked it over, and we'll try you out, twenty of us at five hundred dollars apiece."

Cole felt a new surge of hope. He asked: "Any of you want to hire on as guards? Pay is sixty a month and beans."

Vance Daugherty said: "I'll ride the first half dozen trips, because I'm the one who has talked for you. Now fill your belly with beans and coffee and go get your coach."

VIII

TOO LATE

At nightfall, Cole splashed across the Platte and ten minutes later dismounted at the Elephant Corral. "Feed him good," he told the hosteler. "He's earned it."

He swung around the corner and headed uptown, thinking: *First step is a bath, then a feed. If I feel like it by then, I'll have Doc Fox look at my shoulder.* There was an unaccustomed lightness in his head, and the shoulder and arm throbbed mercilessly. Cole raised it with his right hand and slipped it into the sling Sally Ambrook had fashioned from her shawl. Even yet a hint of Sally's fragrance inhabited the shawl, and Cole smiled a little, remembering her.

As he passed the Quincy House, the door swung open and a voice called: "Cole . . . Mister Estes!" Cole paused, turning. Norah Forrest came onto the walk clad in a dark blue dress with a high collar of white lace. Even in the poor light cast from the windows of the Quincy House, she saw the cutaway sleeve of his buckskin shirt, the dirt and blood on his clothes, the shadow of weariness in his face. Her hand came out and touched his arm lightly.

"You've been hurt."

"Not bad. The bushwhacker's aim wasn't very good."

Concern turned her face sober, her lips soft. Fear touched her wide eyes. "Supposing his aim had been good? Oh, Cole, it isn't worth it. It isn't worth it at all. Please, let's give it up. I have enough money. You can find something to do that will not put your life in danger."

Surprise ran through Cole, and he said: "You've changed

already. It is an old saying that the frontier is tough on women and horses. But I like you better for the change it has made in you."

She laughed unsteadily.

Cole went on: "There are several reasons I'm doing this, and it surprises me to realize that money is the least of them."

"What reason could there be except money?"

"Mike, for one thing. I owe Mike something. Now that I'm started, I find I owe something to the miners on the Vasquez who have put their trust in me."

Norah's eyes dropped, and disappointment put a shadow across her face. Cole thought: *It would not have hurt to tell her she was one of the reasons for doing this . . .* and he realized suddenly that it would have been true.

Norah asked: "You were successful in persuading them that you could transport their gold safely?"

He nodded. Suddenly full awareness came to him of how entirely alone was this girl, how courageously she was facing her loneliness. On impulse he put out his right arm, circled her waist, and drew her to him. She did not resist but, instead, was passive, waiting. Cole bent his head and touched her lips lightly with his own. Drawing back, he said: "It's a rough town now with no place for a girl like you. But that'll change, and you'll be less lonely."

A smile crossed Norah's face, a smile that was older than her years. Standing on tiptoe, she kissed him fully on the lips, then turned, and fled back into the door of the Quincy House.

Cole stood for a moment, looking after her, and then, half smiling, continued toward the Planter's House.

Later, bathed, shaved and fed, a clean dressing on his shoulder, he sought out Hobart, finding him in the lobby of the Planter's House. He sat down so they could talk. Hobart had been busy while Cole was gone. He had sent a rider eastward

74

to Leavenworth, calling in all of the way-station keepers, with instructions to bring all movable equipment and horses. He had hired carpenters and wheelwrights to put into shape what equipment was in Denver City. He had a coach ready for Cole to take in the morning and a driver to hold the reins. Cole said with satisfaction: "You may be a farmer, but you're more than that."

Hobart flushed.

Cole rose. "For some reason tonight the thought of a bed is more welcome than the thought of a bottle. Good night."

He made his way through the crowded lobby and fifteen minutes later, with a chair propped against the door, was asleep.

Dawn found Cole atop the tall seat of a Troy coach, a shotgun held snugly against the seatback by the pressure of his body. Beside him rode the driver, Elston, red-haired, freckled, and salty, and below in the coach rode Hobart. A drunk tottered on the walk beside the McGaa Street bridge, his maudlin song halted while he stared. A swamper tossed a bucket of dirty water into the street from the door of a saloon on Fourth, narrowly missing a man slumped against the wall. The swamper raised a salutary hand as the coach rumbled past, and Cole waved back.

The sun poked above the rim of the eastern plain, laying its copper glow against the jagged line of peaks to the west. On the naked range behind them a thin layer of new snow lay, and Cole remarked to the driver: "They'd better get busy on the Vasquez if they expect to get their gold out before the winter sets in."

"Plenty of time. There will be two full months and a part of another before frost stops 'em."

Drawn by six mules, the coach ran along the dusty road, climbing steadily, and, before mid-morning, reached the Mount

Vernon House, where Cole paid their toll of a dollar and a half that would carry them as far as Cresswell, west of Elk Park.

Now the mules slowed, laboring against their traces as they pulled the weight of the coach up these steep and rocky grades. The coach swayed and strained against its bullhide thorough-braces. So narrow was this road that a dozen times they were forced to pull far to one side to let a wagon or buckboard pass. Men, riding saddle horses and mules, were numerous, and all stared, for this was the first coach they had seen on this road. Occasionally Elston would pass a heavily laden wagon, a freighter bound for the placers on the Vasquez with beans, sugar, coffee, and miner's tools.

With his left arm useless, and giving him pain with every jolt the Troy took, Cole was forced to cling to the seat with his right hand, bracing his feet against the floorboards, and even then there were times when he thought he would be flung clear.

They had their dinner at Cresswell, though it was well after noon when they reached the place, and following this Cole rode inside the coach where he could better brace himself and spare his arm, which was now torturing him to an extent that it blurred his vision and made his head reel. In late afternoon, brakes squealing, they rolled down the long, steep grade into the cañon of the Vasquez.

Vance Daugherty waited with a score of others beside the burnt-out ashes of last night's fire. As Cole climbed out of the coach and approached, he said: "They have changed their minds a dozen times since you were here. They are wondering why they should be the ones to get this plan started, to take all the risk, but I have finally convinced them that conditions will get no better unless someone is willing to take a chance. You and I are gambling our lives. These others have finally agreed to take a chance with their gold."

Cole thought he noted a change in this man since he had

76

last seen him, a certain lack of straightforwardness he had not previously noted. He said: "A vigilante movement has started in Denver City because of the murder of a man named Osten who tried to carry his gold to Denver alone. Eventually his murderers will be known and punished. In the meantime it will be a good thing to let the murderers know that Osten was not the only one who was not afraid of them. Someday a man they try to kill will recognize them and live to tell of it, and that will be the chance for the vigilantes to start their clean up."

Now each man stepped forward to place his gold in the coach's strongbox. This was not gold dust and nuggets carried in pokes but solid chunks of gold that had been fused in the campfire. They were like gleaming pieces of slag from a blast furnace. Each was tagged with its owner's name. When the box was full, Cole closed the lid and snapped the padlock on it.

Hobart and Elston heaved it inside the coach. Cole climbed inside and checked the loads in his Colt. Elston climbed to the seat, sorted his reins, and Hobart climbed up beside him. Vance Daugherty had disappeared, but he came running alongside as the coach got under way and pulled himself in through the door. As he did this, his swinging coat banged against the side of the coach with a thud, as though he carried a pocketful of rocks.

Once inside, he hauled a bottle from his pocket, grinning. "It will be a long ride into Denver City, and this will help pass the time."

Cole felt a stir of anger. He growled: "This is no party but a serious thing. We are sure to be jumped somewhere along the way, and a man with his wits addled by liquor is no good in a fight. Put the damned thing away."

His appreciation for the support this man had given him was rapidly turning to dislike. There was something furtive and insincere about Daugherty that grated against Cole's sense of what a man should be. And, instead of showing anger, as most men would, Daugherty only shrugged, smiled, and settled back against the seat.

Tension began to build in Cole as the coach began its long climb out of the cañon. The road wound interminably back and forth in switchbacks to reduce the grade, and on first one side and then the other the cañon yawned below them, the roar of the Vasquez slowly diminishing as they gained altitude.

At sundown they came to the top of the hill and started down the eastern side. Now Cole could relax somewhat, for here began a long, wide valley through which a tiny stream wandered, and there were no places where they could be ambushed. Out of a corner of his eye he studied Daugherty, wondering about this man.

He said: "It's unusual to find an educated man working a placer. Gold seekers are usually those who have found only failure in their daily lives and are always looking for something to remedy that failure quickly."

Vance Daugherty gave him a twisted grin. He replied: "You think that because a man is educated he's unfamiliar with failure?"

"I had that thought."

Daugherty laughed bitterly. "It's what all men think who don't have an education." His thin face, covered lightly with graying whiskers, showed Cole self-derision, even what appeared to be self-contempt. He added: "Success or failure is determined by what is in the man, not by what he has been taught. Even on the Vasquez I was able to pan only about half as much as the others. But, hell, why talk about me? There must be more pleasant subjects, surely, to pass the time."

Something about Daugherty's words puzzled Cole, but he could not decide what it was. The coach came off this grade, out of the lush meadow, and commenced to climb into heavy timber. The coolness, the dampness of the air here came through the windows of the coach and brought with it the light, pleasant smell of pine. Cole grew tense again, for here, with the coach slowed on the grade and with abundant concealment, an ambush was possible, even likely.

Cole stuck his head close to the window, peering into the increasing gloom ahead. Above him the driver's whip snaked out, popping over the heads of the mules, and Cole could hear Elston's salty stream of curses. Once he glanced about at Daugherty. The man sat stiffly on the edge of his seat, and his face had turned white. His eyes had a peculiar, fixed look, and his hands were held against his knees and could not stay still. Cole said: "Relax, man. It is no use worrying about the thing until it happens."

Turned vaguely uneasy, he drew his Colt and had it on the seat beside him, holding it down and still with his leg. In his mind he was going back over Daugherty's words of a few minutes ago and trying to put his finger on what it was in them that had so puzzled him. Suddenly he yanked his head around to stare at the tall man. He growled: "You said you were able to pan only half as much as the others. Why *were*? Aren't you going back?"

Abruptly now Elston's voice rose atop the coach, and a gun yelped ahead in the timber. A strange voice shouted: "Pull in, driver, or I'll drop you off that box!"

Cole snatched the Colt from under his leg and poked its muzzle through the window. He heard the movement of Daugherty behind him, ignoring it for the moment, and snapped a shot toward the flash in the heavy wall of timber. He heard Elston's whip lay itself sharply against the mules and felt the coach leap forward.

Hobart's shotgun roared above him, and its flash illuminated for an instant the timber and the half dozen horsemen within it. Cole put a shot into the midst of them and was rewarded by a man's harsh yell of pain. Again the shotgun roared, and now gunfire blossomed in the timber. Bullets tore through the thin panels of the coach.

Cole half turned to Daugherty to ask: "What the hell's the matter with you? Ain't you got a gun?"

He caught the man's movement, rising from the seat on the opposite side of the coach, but instead of moving across to the other seat, the man came directly at him. Cole yelled: "Watch what you're doing, damn. . . ." Then he saw Daugherty's upraised arm, saw the long-barreled pistol in the man's hand. He threw himself forward, but, even as he did, he knew he was too late.

The barrel of Daugherty's revolver came down against his skull, bringing an instant of whirling pain and then utter blackness.

IX

STRING 'EM UP!

Dawn was a flaming spectacle of fiery cloud and pale blue sky. The Troy coach stood hidden in the timber no more than two hundred yards from the road, the lead mules tied to a tree. Fidgeting, they sought to lower their heads to graze, but they succeeded only in getting enough to whet their appetites for more. The coach rocked gently back and forth with their movement, and it was this that brought Cole to consciousness and then out of the coach, staggering and blurry-eyed. The first thing he noticed was the overpowering reek of whiskey that rose from his clothes. His confused brain fought for remembrance or understanding of the circumstances that had put him here.

At first he thought: *I must have been on one lulu of a drunk. But how the devil did I get out here?* Then pain brought an exploratory hand to his head. His fingers ran gingerly over the lump there, and slowly he began to recall. He remembered the chest full of gold that had been in the coach. He remembered the attack, the treachery of Vance Daugherty. He growled: "Hobart . . . and Elston? Where the hell are they?"

He made a circle of the coach at a shuffling run that brought dizzying waves of sickness and further pain to his head. Then he headed back along the plain tracks the coach had made in the tall grass, coming at last to the road and to the two silent, cold bodies, lying there, sprawled grotesquely in the dewy grass.

Cole sat down, his stomach contracting spasmodically. He retched, gagged, and almost fainted.

Down the steep grade toward the Vasquez he heard a shout and, plainly then, a man's steady cursing, the creak of an axle, and the metallic jangle of harness. Suddenly it came over him of how this would look. Cole Estes, reeking of whiskey, vomiting, his driver and guard dead on the ground. *God,* he thought, *I've got to have time to think this out.*

He staggered to his feet and, fighting against the pain in his injured arm, dragged first Hobart and then Elston into the timber where they would be hidden from the road. Just in time was he able to hide himself, watching from concealment the passage of an empty freight wagon as it passed on its slow and rumbling way toward Denver City. He held his breath as the wagon lumbered past, keeping an anxious eye on the driver lest he note the signs of disturbance in the grass, but the man was too preoccupied with cursing his mules to give more than a passing glance to the wayside.

As the sound of his cursing faded on the clear morning air, Cole went again to the coach. The chest in which the gold had been locked was splintered and gaping on the ground a dozen yards away. Inside the coach lay Cole's revolver, untouched, and an empty whiskey bottle, one Cole now recognized as the bottle Daugherty had waved at him as he entered the coach on the Vasquez.

Why didn't they kill me too? he asked himself, and for a moment considered the possibility that they'd thought they had. But he shook his head. *They wouldn't be that foolish,* he concluded. *It's got to be something else. If they thought I was dead, why pour whiskey over me?*

It came to him then, and he knew that this was Jess Dyer's way of revenging himself against Cole for the five thousand he had paid out unnecessarily. Dyer had felt killing Cole would afford him only a nominal vengeance. But this . . . ? Cole considered what would now happen. He would drive the coach on into Denver City, carrying the bodies of Elston and Hobart but no gold. He himself would reek of whiskey, would show every evidence of having been on a monstrous drunk. Who, then, would believe his story? Would the miners believe him, those who had lost their gold? Would Norah Forrest believe him, she whose doubt of him had been all too apparent after his interview with Dyer? Her tenuous faith in him would shatter all too easily.

Would the newly organized vigilantes believe that Cole had been sober, that he had been slugged by Daugherty, whom somehow Dyer must have reached and bought in the time it took Cole to return to Denver for the coach? At the very best Cole could expect to be driven from the country, accused of having betrayed everyone who trusted him. At worst he should expect to decorate the handy limb of a cottonwood tree.

The desolation of utter despair washed over him. The only apparent evasion that occurred to him now was mounting one of the mules and fleeing the country. For a short instant he considered this, but then his jaw hardened, and his eyes turned cold. *That is what Dyer wants me to do,* he knew. *Then he'll have a free hand to come in here with his own line.* He began to understand what Daugherty's stake had been: the ten thousand in gold that the coach had been carrying — less, perhaps, the five thousand Dyer had given Norah Forrest — and safe conduct to Denver, maybe even to Leavenworth, with his share of the gold.

Cole thought desperately: *There has got to be someone in Denver who will believe me.* He retrieved his gun from the floor of the coach and began to load it awkwardly from the powder flask at his belt. The shawl sling, used lately only to rest his arm when it was not in use, caught his eye and he pondered: *Sally, I wonder . . . ?* He called to mind the steady clarity of her blue eyes, the softness, the womanliness that was in her.

Fully aware that his story was thin, that it would be difficult for anyone to believe, he nevertheless also knew that this was

83

a chance he had to take. He had to have sanctuary somewhere from which to start his search for Daugherty, who was the key to this thing.

Desperation turned his hands awkward and clumsy as he unharnessed the mules and turned them loose to graze. He thought: *If Sally will not believe me, at least she will not betray me to the vigilantes.* He mounted one of the mules bareback and set out along the road to Denver City at a steady trot, alert for other travelers and ready to leave the road at the first indication of their approach.

It was full dark when Cole came out of the Cherry Creek bottoms and made his cautious way to within a hundred yards of the brightly lighted front of the Gold Coin. Here he found a darkened space between two false-fronted frame buildings and took up his wait for Sally. She would pass within a yard of him on her way to work, unless by some remote chance she came to work by a different route, or unless she was driven there tonight in the carriage of some admirer.

His inactivity and his helplessness made Cole rage inwardly. Every hour that passed meant that Vance Daugherty was putting more miles between himself and Cole Estes. A dozen times during the next hour Cole shrank back into the darkness to avoid discovery by a passerby. This furtiveness further enraged him, and he was in a vicious frame of mind when he finally did see Sally turn the corner and come toward him.

She was dressed tonight in brilliant scarlet, her flaming hair done softly in a bun low on her neck. Over her dress, concealing its scantiness about shoulders and breasts, she wore a light wrap. Cole noticed again tonight, as he had noticed before, the indefinable grace that was in her as she walked. As she drew abreast of his hiding place, he murmured, "Sally?"

Startled, a hand went to her throat, and she poised for an instant like a frightened doe, ready to flee the instant she placed the source of danger.

"Sally, it's me . . . Cole Estes."

Not moving, she asked: "What's the matter? Are you hurt?"

"Worse than that. Will you help me? Will you listen to me?"

There was no hesitation in her, but there was quick fear, and this seemed inexplicably combined with pleasure that he had chosen her to ask for help. She said: "Go back to the alley...to the back door of the Gold Coin. Wait there. I'll come as soon as I can."

Then she was gone, moving rapidly toward the beams of light that fell across the walk from the windows of the Gold Coin. Cole walked through the velvety dark, stumbling over scrap lumber, and shortly stopped before the Gold Coin's back door. He waited only an instant. Then the door opened, and Sally whispered in the darkness, "Come on. Take my hand or you'll stumble."

He closed her small, warm hand within his own, and she led him up a stairway and out into the dimly lighted hall on the second floor. "One more flight," she whispered, and again they climbed stairs. Sally opened a door, and only then did she speak normally as she drew him inside. "Are you in trouble? Is someone after you?"

"Not yet."

Sally struck a match and held it to the lamp that stood on the table, lowering the rose-colored shade over the flame and turning it low. She looked at him, and her face mirrored compassion and something else, something that put the innocence of a young girl into her eyes. "You've been hurt again."

Cole was now very conscious of his appearance, of the dirty stubble that covered his face, of the dried blood that matted his hair, most of all of the reek of whiskey that still clung to his clothes. But these things seemed to matter not at all to Sally. Softly perfumed, she moved near to him. Suddenly he closed her in his arms, and she pressed herself against him, raising eager and slightly parted lips. She said wonderingly: "You're in trouble, and you've come to me. Why didn't you go to that other girl . . . Norah Forrest?"

"You'll know when you hear the story." Cole released her and stepped back. His face turned bitter. "I wouldn't believe it myself if I didn't know it was true."

He sank into a chair upholstered in tapestry, the weariness of the last two days beginning to make itself felt. "I started a run between here and the Vasquez. I persuaded some miners to ship their gold to Denver, but the stage was held up before we got to Cresswell and the gold stolen."

Sally interrupted: "That's easy to believe. There're hold-ups all the time."

"You haven't heard it all. The driver and guard were killed. I was inside the coach because it was easier on my shoulder and arm. With me inside the coach was a miner who helped persuade the others to take a chance with their gold. Instead of fighting, he slugged me and poured whiskey over me." Cole's voice rose involuntarily, "They killed the others, but they didn't kill me. They tried to make it look as though I was drunk and didn't put up a fight."

Cole was angry. He was angry because of what Dyer was trying to do to him, but more than that he was angry because of Elston and especially because of Hobart, who'd been expecting help from inside the stage and had gotten none. He watched Sally closely, waiting for the shadow of doubt upon her face, but he saw only surprise.

She said softly: "I have seen you only twice, and yet I believe you. But a woman's heart and the minds of men are different things. The vigilantes are new, and this will be the first crime committed since their organization. You mustn't let them find you."

Cole's mind was running ahead, and he spoke his thoughts aloud. "If I was Dyer and had put Daugherty up to this thing, I'd sure as hell not want him found. I'd kill him, or I'd hold him somewhere, but I'd not let him out of Denver City until this thing was settled."

"Then you've got to find Daugherty."

Cole answered her bitterly: "And how can I do that? If I stick my head out of this door, they'll grab me. They failed to catch the men who killed George Osten. Do you think I'll get a fair shake if they catch me? It's too easy to say . . . 'He's lying! String him up!' "

With no hesitation whatever Sally said: "You can stay here. I'll bring you food."

"Marple helped organize the vigilantes. He'll find out and turn me in."

"He'll be quiet if I ask him to. He'll believe you because I believe you."

Cole glanced at her sharply, beginning to understand Marple — and Sally as well. He said: "I've no right to ask this of you." He stood up.

She came close to him and slipped her arms about his waist. She explained, her eyes still and honest, "John Marple is in love with me, but it hasn't been like that for me. Can you believe that . . . ?" Halting, she dropped her eyes. Color ran across her cheeks.

Ignoring the pain in his arm, Cole brought her roughly against him. Her arms slipped up to his neck, and she raised her lips to his. Excitement and passion were inexorably combined with tenderness as Cole felt the eager pressure of her. His face buried itself in her fragrant, flaming hair, and his lips found the soft hollow where her neck and shoulder joined. Sally gave a small, helpless cry. Then, suddenly, Cole's passion ended as quickly as it had kindled. He pushed away from her, breathing hoarsely. "No, by God! It's the man who should be giving, not forever taking." He strode to the window and scowled, looking into the street.

Sally's eyes upon him were dark and unreadable for an instant. Then she smiled, and Cole did not see the shining pride that came in a flash to her face and left as quickly, to be replaced by a woman's unending doubt. The words — "Is it Norah Forrest?" — were never uttered. Sally stood for a moment, watching him, and then she said: "First of all, you will need a bath and clean clothes. Then we'll see what can be done about finding this Daugherty. John will help us there. I know he'll help us."

She was rewarded by Cole's look of puzzled gratitude. He said: "Another woman would have been angry."

She turned away so that he couldn't see her face. But she was thinking: *Another woman would not love you so much that nothing mattered to her but what you wanted.* She closed the door behind her and went to find John Marple, knowing in her heart that this was all wrong, that no woman had the right to ask of a man who loved her what she was now going to ask of John Marple. Yet, there was no hesitation in her at all, for she was a woman not plagued by uncertainty once she had decided what must be done.

X

THE LONG MOMENT

Wearing his perpetual scowl of bitterness, the scowl which he had worn since the night George Osten's body had been buried, Karl Osten slouched down Blake toward Cherry Creek. He was a tall and towheaded boy, thin from denying the voracious and unending hunger of youth, the hunger that was never satisfied because there was never quite enough money. His first sharp grief at the loss of his father had lessened, but there were times yet, like today, when sudden awareness that he was entirely alone would turn him sullen and defiant.

Wandering alone in the creek bottoms had its way of easing his tortured thoughts, for he was yet boy enough to find the small creatures who lived there of extreme interest. There were minnows in the shallow pools; there were frogs, rabbits, squirrels, even an occasional coyote or deer, though these were to be seen only at dusk or in early morning. There was peace in the soft voice of the creek, in the quiet rustling of the cottonwood leaves overhead. Here, alone with his back to a tree, anything became possible to Karl, even the money for passage across the sea to bring his mother to this new country, even the discovery and punishment of his father's killer.

So down the creek Karl wandered, his path zigzagging aimlessly, and at noon he halted and sat down, hungry but reluctant to return to the small shack that he now occupied together with his father's friend. Nearly hidden in willow brush, he was startled as a man walked past, carrying a sack over his shoulder. The man was bearded and dirty, but it was his furtiveness that made Karl shrink out of sight until he had passed. It was the same furtiveness that aroused the boy's curiosity and drew him along behind the stranger at a safe distance.

A quarter mile westward, very near the place where Cherry Creek flowed into the Platte, the man entered a small log cabin and closed the door behind him. Karl's curiosity was waning, but, nevertheless, he sat down and concealed himself in the brush to watch.

This cabin was small, hastily and carelessly built. Where its oiled-paper windows had once been were now rough boards, and weeds, grown high about the door, indicating that it had until very recently been abandoned, perhaps by a miner gone for the summer to the mines.

Karl gave it his fleeting attention and then lay back to daydream of the things he would do when he found his father's killer. He was a helpless and lonely boy no longer, but a man, grown tall and strong. Muscles bulged inside his tight shirt, and a gun swung at his hip. Respect showed in the faces of the people he passed on the street, and in his imagination he heard a man murmur, "That's Karl Osten. He's found out who murdered his father, and he's going into that saloon to kill him."

The saloon doors banged open as he thrust his way inside. At the bar, a lone man whirled, his face losing color and turning gray. Karl snarled: "Murderer!" — waiting, knowing the pattern of these things, knowing that the man had to fight.

Like a cornered animal then, yellowed teeth showing, the man at the bar flung a lightning hand toward his gun. It came out, spitting flame. Bullets whined close to Karl's head. Smiling grimly, Karl drew his own gun and fired. The man let out a scream and dropped. . . .

Down at the cabin a door slammed. Karl started and sat up, realizing suddenly that his forehead was bathed with sweat.

The bearded, furtive man was leaving, the sack, empty and

dangling from his hand. This puzzled Karl. He had no way of knowing what had been in the sack, but, whatever it was, it was now inside the cabin.

The man passed him, fifty feet away. As soon as the sound of his movement through the brush had stopped, Karl rose and walked cautiously toward the small and deserted cabin. For no apparent or tangible reason fear touched him as he drew close, made him hesitate, nearly made him turn away. But the day-dream of courage and strength was yet with him, and he forced himself on.

At one side of the cabin a board had been torn away from a window, and it was to this opening that Karl went. Crouching beneath it, he heard a sound within the cabin that sent a chill down his spine. His breathing turned loud and hurried. Carefully he raised himself until he could peep inside.

A man sat in the center of the room at a crude table, eating, his back to Karl. He was a tall man, thin and somewhat stooped. His clothes were ragged, yet there was, in the way he ate, a certain elegance that reminded Karl of people he had seen eating in the Planter's House.

Food, then, had been in the sack. Still, it was puzzling to Karl that this man would be here, apparently well and unhurt, having his food carried to him so far and in such a furtive manner. He backed from the window, worrying at his puzzlement with only a part of his mind, with the rest thinking of his own dinner, now an hour delayed, and feeling the increasing pangs of hunger.

Shrugging lightly at the peculiar actions of men, he left his place at the window and started his long walk back toward town. He hurried because he was hungry. He had not gone two hundred yards before the bearded one stepped from behind a tree, querying roughly: "Where you goin' so fast, snoopy?" He reached a long arm out to grab him.

Instinctively Karl began to run, dodging the reaching hand nimbly. The man lumbered along behind him, fast enough in his clumsy way, slowly closing the lead Karl had gained by his surprised first spurt of speed.

Karl resorted to dodging, to diving into thick clumps of brush and trying to outthink his pursuer. But the bearded man seemed always just a thought ahead of him, and the lead he had narrowed even more.

Panic touched Karl. His chest heaved and fought for air. His breathing grew fast and hoarse. His legs became weights, and his throat was on fire.

He scrambled out of the creek bottom at Blake, the man now only fifty feet behind him. Recklessly he cut in ahead of a lumbering wagon, and behind him the man had to swerve. By this maneuver Karl gained ten feet. He crashed through a cloister of men on the walk, bowling one to the ground, and his pursuer lost another several feet in avoiding their outstretched and irate hands.

Ahead, the splendor of the Gold Coin loomed, and Karl saw a woman alighting from a carriage. He dodged, but she stepped into his path, and he knocked her against the carriage driver, skinning his nose when he fell himself. On hands and knees he saw his pursuer approaching, slowing because of his sureness, his face ugly with rage and streaming sweat.

Karl yelled: "I ain't done nothin'! I just looked in an old cabin window an' seen a man eatin'. But he started chasin' me."

Sally Ambrook smiled. The coachman growled: "You little hellion! I'll learn you to go runnin' around, knockin' ladies down!"

Karl howled: "Please! I didn't mean to. Don't let him get me!"

He stumbled to his feet, but his yelling had taken all of the breath that remained to him. He knew he could run no more.

The bearded man seized him roughly, and cuffed his mouth with the back of a hairy hand. Sally's voice was icy. "Take your hands off that boy!"

The carriage driver moved close, interfering in this because of Sally. "You heard her, mister! Let him go." The inevitable crowd began to collect. Hating his own weakness, Karl began to blubber, fear and exhaustion both contributing to the sobs that tore at his throat.

Sally said again: "Let him go!" Now men from the crowd moved forward to enforce her demand. The bearded man snarled viciously, but he released Karl's arm and backed away.

Sally caught at Karl's sleeve and murmured, "Go inside until you're rested. Then we'll see what this is all about."

Sally Ambrook followed the weary and panting boy into the cool dimness that was the Gold Coin at midday. At first her interference had been prompted only by pity for this boy's fear and exhaustion. But then a small memory had stirred within her, and recognition of his pursuer had come. The bearded man had been present the night Rupp had fought with Cole Estes. He had been one of those cheering Rupp on. Perversity and antagonism had thenceforth controlled Sally, but, as she listened to the boy's hurried and breathless story, she began to wonder if he had not unwittingly uncovered the thing that might in the end defeat Rupp and Dyer and save Cole. For his description of the man at the cabin tallied with Cole's description of Daugherty. Too, it seemed odd that one of Rupp's cronies would be carrying food to a hidden man, unless that man were Daugherty.

Quick elation made Sally hurry the boy upstairs, made her tremulous and hopeful, after leaving him in the room with Cole, while she returned downstairs to get the boy some dinner. Later, when she brought a plate of steaming venison for the boy into

Cole's room, the boy had obviously already told Cole what he had seen. Cole was excited and jubilant.

"Sally, this is it!" he said to her, as she took the plate to the boy who was sitting at the small table. "They've got Daugherty down there at that cabin now, but they won't keep him there long. I've got to get to him before they have time to take him somewhere else."

Sally set the plate down before the boy, smiled her encouragement, and watched him as he began to eat, timidly and slowly at first, but with increasing ravenousness.

Cole said: "Hang it, Sally, you're not listening."

She gave Cole her full attention now, feeling his excitement touch her with its contagion. He was buckling on the Navy Colt and belt. Depression and defeat were gone from him, and in their place was this new enthusiasm and strong male-animal recklessness.

She said: "It's full daylight. How will you get there without being seen?"

"I don't give a hang if I'm seen. All I want is to get my two hands on that. . . ." He paused. "Once I get to Daugherty, then the vigilantes can have us both." He moved toward the door.

A sudden fear chilled Sally, and she pleaded: "Let John go with you. Wait until I can find him. Please! Do at least that for me."

He shrugged, his disappointment plain, but he also realized just how much he owed to this woman. "All right. But hurry. Rupp won't waste any time getting to Daugherty once he realizes that we know where he is."

Sally ran from the room. Five minutes later she watched as Cole and John Marple mounted horses in the alley behind the Gold Coin and spurred recklessly toward Cherry Creek. Sally Ambrook had learned to care for herself in a land full of vio-

94

lence. She had been often afraid, but never quite so afraid as she now was. Trembling, she closed the door, and for a long moment stood with her back against it before she climbed the stairs.

XI

THEY'LL BE BACK

Marple led the way, never leaving this alley until he came to the creek. A steep path led downward here into the creek bottoms, and the two turned their horses and spurred them westward along the wide and sandy bottom that had been formed ages past by the rampaging waters in springtime.

In his careful and cautious way Marple managed to avoid the tent settlements that lay scattered in the cottonwoods, and Cole was suddenly thankful for the man's company, knowing that he himself would have forgotten caution entirely in the urgency of the moment.

There was no mistaking the cabin to which Karl had referred, for it was the only permanent building within half a mile of the place where Cherry Creek entered the Platte. In a fringe of cottonwoods a hundred yards away John Marple halted, holding his fidgeting horse with difficulty. He warned: "He may have a gun, so we'd better leave the horses here and go in on foot."

Cole grinned. "I've got a better idea. We may need these horses. You stay here while I go in. When I'm inside the cabin, you tie the horses. I know Dyer's careful way. Knowing that Daugherty's presence here is known, he'll lose no time in moving him and hiding him somewhere else."

There was a certain unspoken antagonism between these two. Cole recognized it for what it was, animal rivalry over Sally Ambrook, masked but lightly by a civilized control. Marple nodded his grudging assent.

Sun beat downward, hot in this airless and brushy bottom. Sweat dampened Cole's shirt, and excitement stirred him as he made his swift but careful way from tree to tree, from brushy pocket to brushy pocket. At last he stood but a short stone's throw from the cabin door. If not for the need to extract a confession from Daugherty, Cole would have called to him now, would have fought it out across this narrow stretch of grass that lay before the cabin door. Realizing, however, that vindication for himself lay in Daugherty's spoken words, he cat-footed across the clearing. Coming to the door, he flung it wide and entered with a rush, gun in hand.

Daugherty, reading an old newspaper that he had spread out on the table, sprang to his feet, whirling, entirely surprised and unprepared. Seeing Cole, his hand snaked foolishly toward the gun at his side, but Cole rushed forward and brought his own gun barrel smashing down across Daugherty's wrist.

Daugherty howled with pain, and a grin of pleasure crossed Cole's twisted and enraged face. His hand went out toward Daugherty's undrawn gun. When the man dodged, this time he brought his own Colt smashing against the side of Daugherty's face. Daugherty staggered. His hand went to his face, came away sticky and red with blood.

Cole said harshly: "The gun. Hand it over and be careful, or I'll give you this one again in the same place. Marple will be here in a minute, and then you're going to talk. You're going to tell everything you know, and you're going to tell us exactly what happened the other night."

"They kidnapped me! They slugged me, and I couldn't help you! I swear that's the truth. I swear it!"

Again Cole swung his gun. The barrel and the cylinder smashed again into the bloody side of Daugherty's face. As Daugherty staggered, Cole yanked the man's gun from its holster and flung it, sliding, across the floor. His voice was cold. "The trouble with thieves is that they think honest men are soft. I'll show you how soft I am. Are you going to talk, or do you want this again in the same place?" He heard the door close behind him and swung his head to look at Marple. "He'll talk, but don't interfere." Now he asked of Daugherty: "How much did they pay you to slug me on the stage?"

Vance Daugherty hesitated, but, as Cole advanced with the gun in his fist, he babbled: "Two thousand, but it should have been more. There was thirty thousand in the box."

"Who paid you, Rupp or Dyer?"

"They haven't paid me yet. And they got my gold along with the rest."

"Who held up the stage?"

"It was Rupp. He's the one that's been robbing the miners on the Vasquez. He's the one that killed Osten."

Cole laughed harshly. "You're a fool! Do you think they'd let you live, knowing that about them? Do you really think they'd give you back your gold or pay you for slugging me? There's only one reason that you're alive now, and that's because you might be useful as a witness against me."

Marple interjected a question: "Where does Dyer fit in?"

Daugherty replied: "He's behind Rupp. When he's driven Estes out of business, he'll haul the miners' gold, but there'll still be enough of it stolen to make the hauling profitable. And he'll raise the rates for hauling it to twenty percent."

Cole grinned, asking Marple: "Heard enough?"

Marple nodded.

Cole turned toward the door, yanking Vance Daugherty with him. The horses had wandered as far as the first fringe of brush. Marple moved ahead now, toward them, and, as he did, a bullet thumped behind Cole and Daugherty into the soft log wall of the cabin. The report made a flat and vicious sound in the still, hot air.

Cole growled to Daughtery: "Run, damn you, but don't try to get away. If they don't get you, I will."

Daughtery drove across the open clearing, his legs pumping furiously, but he tripped as he neared the brush and slid on his face. When he came to hands and knees, the bloody side of his face was encrusted with sand, and his face was twisted with pain. There was no pity in Cole. Pity was killed by his thinking of Elston and Hobart, dead because of this man's treachery and lust for gold.

Cole entered the thicket with a rush, as bullets ripped into the ground behind him, kicking up their spurts of fine sand. Marple was holding the horses, prancing and frantic, and Cole said sharply to Daugherty, pointing to his mount: "Hoist yourself up, and fast!"

Daughtery scrambled into the saddle, and Cole snatched the reins from Marple, leaping up behind Daugherty. Marple mounted his own horse easily and swiftly, and this way they pounded into the open and up the bank southward, angling across the grass toward the road.

Behind, half a dozen riders boiled out of the bottoms, firing over their galloping horses' heads.

Daugherty yelled, his voice rising on a note of terror: "They'll kill us!"

Cole shouted into his ear: "Hell, nobody can shoot straight from a running horse. You just better hope that none of them gets the idea of stopping and using a rifle."

The distance into town, so long to a boy afoot, was a matter of minutes to men atop galloping horses. At the Gold Coin they yanked to a sliding halt, piling off and releasing the horses to move off upstreet uncertainly, reins dragging. Cole shoved Daugherty into the door, crowded Marple after him, saying: "Watch him. He'll get away if he can." He turned then, his lips splitting into a savage grin. As the pursuers rounded the corner, he brought up the smooth-worn Navy Colt and let a shot rip downstreet toward the creek. A man yelled and came tumbling from his saddle.

This brought the lot of them to a chaotic halt, and their shooting from the backs of their plunging horses was no match for Cole's steady aim. Cole fired again, dropping a second man. His third shot went through the neck of one of the horses, and the animal went down, pinning his rider beneath his twitching body.

As quickly as they had come into it, they whirled from the street and went out of sight. Behind, they left two still shapes and a yelling, struggling man, trapped beneath a dead horse.

Cole backed into the Gold Coin and heard Marple's worried voice: "They'll be coming again. We've got the thing that'll bust their gang wide open. I'm going out to round up the vigilantes. We'll never have a better chance to clean out Rupp's crew."

He ran through the door, but a shot ripped into the frame wall beside him, and he ducked swiftly back. Cole said: "They didn't run. They're covering the door from the corner with rifles. Try the back."

Together they ran through the big room, and now Daugherty followed, craven and thoroughly frightened. Sally met them there at the door. "The alley is full of men. I barred the door."

Cole shrugged.

Marple said: "The vigilantes'll hear the shooting."

Sally was more realistic. "Half of the men in the alley belong to the vigilantes." Her face was strickened and frightened, and it held her knowledge of how this would end. Confusion was allied with Rupp's forces. The vigilantes would be disorganized, easily persuaded that this attack was for the sole purpose of killing or capturing Cole Estes, whom Marple was hiding in the Gold Coin.

Marple asked: "What will they do now?"

Cole looked at Sally, so soft and wide-eyed, so filled with

fear. He would not say what was in his thoughts, but he knew how ruthless Jess Dyer could be. Here was one way of eliminating all of the opposition in one terrible operation. Jess Dyer would not overlook it. Of that Cole was certain. Coal oil and fire would do for Jess Dyer what the guns of his toughs could not.

It was an accurate prophecy. Presently flames were licking at the walls of the towering and imposing Gold Coin. The walls were dry and fire-hungry. Heat forced the four up the stairs, but it was not until they reached the third floor that Cole remembered Karl Osten.

"Where's the boy?"

Concern sent Sally running from room to room. When she came back, there was puzzlement in her expression, but also there was elation and gladness that in some way the boy had been spared this death by fire. "Poor kid. He must've been afraid even of staying here. He must've run out the front door while you were trying to leave by the back."

The fire in the lower portion of the building now made a steady roar, and the rising heat was becoming unbearable. Minutes only remained to them, Cole knew. He went to the window and began firing methodically into the street. Useless perhaps, but it was very necessary to him that this should cost Dyer something. He saw the look that passed between Sally and Marple, and suddenly self-blame flooded over him, because it was he who had brought them to this. Swiftly he began to rip bedsheets into strips, knotting these strips together into a long rope. He would die by a bullet, perhaps, before he could reach the ground, but at least he would not die helplessly.

XII

THE RIGHTEOUS ANGER

Karl Osten had known by the very urgency and concern that was in Cole Estes that his discovery of the man in the cabin had an importance greater than any that was at first apparent. He was grateful to Sally for rescuing him from the bearded man, yet she was a stranger and, as such, could not entirely quiet the fear that was beginning to consume him. He sensed that there was real danger in the thing he had discovered. To the strongest of mortals danger is most easily faced from familiar surroundings.

As soon as Sally went downstairs when they heard the sound of shots in the street, Karl followed quietly. When Cole and Marple hurried to the back door with the fugitive he had seen, Karl slipped out the front. He dodged a bullet sent at him from a man hidden around the corner, then he was out of range across the street. He had gone little over a block when he noticed a man following him, closing the distance between them rapidly. Karl ducked into a narrow passageway between two buildings, ran, and, when he came to the back alley, turned and lost himself in a pile of empty crates and rubbish. Crouching there, he saw the man come into the alley and shortly saw him meet with two others who had entered from either end of the alley. The three stood, talking quietly, and Karl caught the words: "He's hiding here somewhere. You two cover the ends of the alley, and I'll look around. Rupp'll nail our hides to the barn door if that kid gets to the vigilantes."

Trembling, Karl waited. He could hear the man poking around in the rubbish pile, drawing nearer. A rat scurried past

102

him, pausing momentarily to stare at him with beady, unwinking eyes. The man kicked a can, and it rolled to within inches of Karl's feet. Jumping up, he leaped atop the piled crates, fell, felt the man's clutching hand. Then he slipped away, darted up two flights of open stairway, and ran into a dim hall. A door was open into a room to his right, and he went through this, coming to a window that faced onto the roof of an adjoining building. A drop of ten feet yawned below the window, but Karl lowered himself until he was hanging by his hands, and then dropped. Gravel crunched under his feet. Above, he could hear the sound as his pursuer pounded into the hall.

Karl ran, and then crouched behind a chimney half way across the flat roof. He trembled as he heard the man's cursing voice from the window, and he waited in terror for the sound that would tell him the man had dropped from it.

The sound did not come, and he heard the man's retreating steps, heard a door slam, heard baffled and obscene cursing, muffled by distance. Below in the alley one of the others called: "Get him, Sam?"

Sam yelled down: "Hell, he's here somewhere. It's a ten foot drop out of this window. Come on up here an' give me a hand."

For what seemed an eternity, Karl crouched there, unmoving. His legs turned stiff and began to tingle from poor circulation, yet he would not move. He could see the towering Gold Coin across the street, and, after what he judged to be several minutes, he heard voices again in the alley. "That kid just disappeared! Let's get the hell out of here. As long as Rupp don't know he got away, we'll be all right, so don't say anything."

It was then that more shots sounded in the street, mingled with the frantic pound of galloping hoofs. Taking his chance, Karl crept to the edge of the roof, peeping over the low parapet to look into the street. He saw Cole Estes drop two men and a horse with three deliberate shots. Still Karl waited. He saw Rupp's men run into the street from both ends, and he saw the blaze of the fire and, once, Sally's white and frightened face at an upstairs window.

To Karl this suddenly abrupt daylight violence was shockingly unreal, and fear for his own life brought a quick trembling over him that made his teeth chatter. Fear had touched him before while he was being chased. But it had not been this icy and raw fear for his life. In panic, he ran to the back edge of the roof.

He scanned the alley from one end to the other, but he saw no one, for the excitement in the street had drawn everyone there. A lean-to shack provided a quick and easy way to the ground, and five minutes later Karl pounded into the tiny one-room shack on the eastern outskirts of town.

The fat man forced quiet and coherence into the terrified boy by sternness and patience. When he had the story, he took down the long flintlock rifle from the wall. "Come with me, Karl. We will see what the vigilantes will do now. If they will do nothing, then at least you and I can do our bit against these murderers." He handed Karl the pistol that had been his father's and led the way at a swift and panting walk toward town.

There is something grimly terrible about the righteous anger of honest men. Cole saw them coming, in tightly compact groups from either end of the street, as he swung himself from the window and began his sliding descent to the ground. With his head level with the window, he told Sally: "If it will hold my weight, it will hold yours. Wait until the shooting stops and then come down."

The knots slowed him, and bullets cut viciously into the frame walls beside him. Concentrating only on speeding his descent, he heard the vicious chatter of gunfire as the vigilantes

104

opened up on the concealed, sniping toughs. He felt a slamming blow against his left arm, the burn of pain, and the wetness of blood. The arm lost all of its strength in a single, numbing instant, and Cole slid unchecked for a full five feet until his right hand caught on one of the knots. In that short instant a scream rose from the street below. Holding on, sweating, Cole glanced around, saw the upturned and terrified face of Norah Forrest.

Her scream was not heard by himself alone. He saw the monstrous and long-armed figure of Rupp running, saw him seize the girl, saw the brief struggle and the brutal blow of Rupp's fist that turned her limp and silent.

Rage flamed in his brain, and he released the crude rope, dropping the last ten feet and feeling the shock of falling, the momentary dizziness as he hit the ground. Rupp was fleeing, the form of Norah tossed across his shoulder.

From the window above he heard Sally's scream: "Cole!" He yanked his glance around, tilting his face upward. Sally was sliding down the rope, and above her John Marple's face was a mask of horrified concern. Cole glanced around once more, the awfulness of indecision tearing at him. Rupp had disappeared, and his disappearance with Norah Forrest gave Cole the answer he had been seeking, but, loving Norah or not, he could not leave until Sally was safe on the ground.

He waited then, catching her in his arms before her feet could touch the ground. In an instant John Marple was down, and Daugherty came immediately behind him. Cole released Sally, who gave his face an instant's searching, then turned wordlessly to Marple. Marple tossed Cole a triumphant look, closing Sally in his arms, and Cole grinned. Then he whirled, running, heading for the Planter's House and the offices of the I. C. & K. T. Express. Norah Forrest was Rupp's hostage, but, when Rupp left the country, he would want his gold, and he would need a coach in which to travel.

Cole fought his way through the ranks of vigilantes, through the crowd of curious onlookers. Fire-fighting equipment was moving up, ladders, wagons loaded with tanks and buckets, and this further slowed him. There was in Cole a feeling of time forever lost, and desperation turned him frantic. For the moment Norah was useful to Rupp, for she guaranteed his escape. Later, when he had made good his escape. . . .

At a tearing run Cole rounded the last corner, and even from here he could see the still form that lay on the walk before the Planter's House. Upstreet, a coach swayed and rocked as its galloping horses took it swiftly out of town, heading eastward along the road toward Leavenworth.

Cole paused for a brief instant beside the body that lay on the walk. Jess Dyer, in death, still showed the evil and ugliness that had been so apparent in him in life. Cole was reminded of his own words to Dyer: "You can die as quickly as any man." He knew that Dyer had never believed it until perhaps the last moment when Rupp fired the fatal shot.

Beside the body lay a small trunk, spilled open, its contents plainly Dyer's clothes and personal belongings. Cole muttered, "You were skipping with the gold, and Rupp caught you. Now he's got the gold, and he's got Norah, too."

The rack before the hotel held half a dozen drowsing horses, and Cole picked a tall and glossy black, swinging into the saddle as the horse broke into his run. His left arm had scarcely the strength to hold the reins, but he would need his right for the revolver. His heels drummed on the black's sides, urging the speeding animal to even greater exertion. The coach was only a speck ahead, lost in its rising dust cloud.

The grain-fed horse began to sweat, but Cole slowly closed the distance between himself and the coach. While he was yet a hundred yards behind, Rupp opened fire with his rifle, using it one-handed from atop the Concord.

Cole, helpless to return the fire because of Norah inside and because of the uncertainty of shooting from the back of a running horse, was forced to face Rupp's deadly fire with only the swerving of his horse from side to side to throw it off. Then the gap had closed until he was directly behind the coach and sheltered from Rupp's fire by the Concord itself. Still there was no sign of Norah.

Cole drew slowly ahead on the right side of the coach and, peering inside, saw the sprawled and unconscious form of Norah, half on the seat, half on the floor, being pounded mercilessly from side to side by the rocking of the coach. He drew farther ahead until he could see Rupp, his hands full now with the bolting teams, but holding them with his left hand only, while his right turned a revolver toward Cole.

The flame and smoke from Rupp's gun were acrid and blinding in Cole's face, but the bullet had missed him. Cole raised his own gun and, as the sights wobbily centered on Rupp's naked and hairy chest, snapped off a shot.

The big man howled, a roar of mingled pain and shock, stood up on the seat, and pitched off directly in front of Cole's galloping horse. Cole felt the lift as the black soared over Rupp and was nearly unseated by the shock and surprise of it. The coach had drawn ahead in this short instant, but Cole drummed on the black's wet sides and forced him abreast.

This was the vicious part — Norah unconscious, terrified, with runaway teams drawing the lumbering coach, Cole himself with only one good arm. He holstered the Colt, swung his right leg over the black's neck, braced it momentarily against the saddle, and leaped. The black veered away, and for a split second Cole hung in mid-air, the whirling, grinding wheels of the coach directly beneath him, reaching and hungry.

He felt his hand, his right hand, close on the seat rail. His left met it, but his feet were dangling and touched momentarily the spokes of the front wheel. Slowly and painfully he drew himself up, and at last sat atop the bounding seat.

The reins, dropped by Rupp as he had stood up, dragged now on the ground between the teams. Cole leaped from the seat, landing astride one of the wheelers, and, clinging to harness, leaned far to one side, finally grasping the trailing reins.

He straightened then, hauling back with all his strength. Slowly, slowly the horses came under his control, until he could draw them to a full halt, could climb back into the seat, and set the brake.

He was down then and into the coach. Norah, bleeding slightly from her bruised mouth, was stirring and moaning, but she clung to him and drew herself close.

There was time for relief and time for thankfulness. The Osten boy would have his father's gold. The vigilantes would have Daugherty and the remainder of Rupp's gang. The time for hunger and for love would come later, when Denver City was peaceful again.